MAN ROBS BANK WITH HIS CHIN

AND OTHER UNUSUAL STORIES MISSED BY MAINSTREAM MEDIA

By Jeffrey L. Gurian

Jeffrey@jeffreygurian.com

www.comedymatterstv.com

Copyright © 2016 by Jeffrey Gurian.
All rights reserved. No part of this publication may be reproduced, distributed, or transmitted in any form or by any means, including photocopying, recording, or other electronic or mechanical methods, without the prior written permission of the publisher, except in the case of brief quotations embodied in critical reviews and certain other noncommercial uses permitted by copyright law.

For permission requests, write to the publisher, addressed "Attention: Permissions Coordinator," at the address below:
Happiness Center Publications
P.O.Box 7267
F.D.R. Station
New York, NY 10022

ISBN 978-1-7354426-2-4

Happiness Center Publications

Printed in the United States of America

ABOUT THE AUTHOR

We live in a strange and unusual world, in which things happen that are beyond our comprehension. Some of them are so interesting and unusual you might think they had to be made up!

And even stranger, most of the time we don't even hear about them. Jeffrey Gurian's mission in life seems to be to counteract that. As a former writer/reporter for the legendary *Weekly World News*, he started out reporting on stories like "Tap Dancing For The Criminally Insane," "Man Paints Replica of the Sistine Chapel With His Beard," and "College Professor Fired For Casually Removing His Spine."

Shortly afterwards he wound up with his own column called "Gurian's World of the Bizarre" featuring stories like "Rare Virus Sweeps Japan, Victims Too Weak To Bow," "Man Impaled On Spike Still Shows Up For Work On Time," and "Mexican Hat Dance Adopted By Sweden." It can be said that Jeffrey Gurian has always been fascinated by very unusual stories.

This led him to launch *GNN, Gurian News Network*, which he considers to be your source for "All The News That's Fit To Dance To," and which covers the most unusual stories in the world missed by mainstream media.

In his spare time he is also an inventor who is responsible for inventions that have changed the world, like the flashlight that works during the day, (so now people can see where they're going during the day too), the 24 hour stapler, (for people who enjoy stapling things late into the night), and the battery-operated beard, (as opposed to the old kind you had to plug in, because hot models often like men with Biblical length beards that swing like a pendulum,), as well as the reversible beard for men who travel and want to pack light, but still want to have a change of beard when they get where they're going.

Gurian claims not to have slept at all since he was a child. He just stays up all night searching the entire world for the most unusual stories he can find. He also spends much of his time reminiscing. He reminisces about people he's never met, places he's never gone, and things he's never done before.

"Sometimes," he says, "I just sit around thinking about all the parking spots I've ever found and who's parked in them now. Then I think about all the wrong numbers I've ever received and wonder what those people are doing. And then I think maybe we should have kept in touch. And then I contemplate all the people I passed on the escalator going down while I was going up, and wonder how they've been doing."

This will give you some insight as to why Jeffrey felt the need to write this book. Some of you may never sleep again!

FOREWORD by Scott Dikkers

I'm somewhat responsible for the modern flood of pseudo-news comedy. I founded theonion.com in the mid 1990s, which led to many imitators and inspired (and staffed) a lot of the comedy news TV shows that started showing up on TV in the 2000s. But before that, before even *The Onion* newspaper (founded in 1988), there were only three news outlets in America dedicated to news-based comedy: *Weekend Update*, supermarket tabloids, and HBO's *Not Necessarily the News*. That's it. *Weekend Update* and *Not Necessarily the News* did traditional comedy, billed as such, performed in front of a live audience (or maybe, in the case of *Not Necessarily the News*, a laugh track—I'm not sure). They were nothing out of the ordinary.

The supermarket tabloids were different. And by "supermarket tabloids" I don't mean the *National Enquirer* and the other hunt-the-celebrity circulars. I'm talking about a special kind of tabloid: the newspaper parody. *The Sun*, and *The Weekly World News* were the best. They were unique not just among the other supermarket tabloids, they were unique among any publications that did parody, including *Mad Magazine*, the *National Lampoon* and *Spy*.

What set the news tabloids apart was that nowhere did they say, "this is a parody." Not under the masthead, not in the staff listing or copyright, not with a red banner on the upper corner of the cover that said "parody!," which a lot of books did in those days, thus destroying the conceit (and therefore the fun) for readers. They behaved like serious news sources. Their fonts were serious. Their photos were serious, at least, as serious as they could be before the advent of Photoshop.

These trailblazing publications tested readers' ability to tell the real from the made-up, and they confused and deluded untold millions waiting in line at the supermarket the same way *The Onion* gets credit for deluding people today.

The golden age of the *Weekly World News* and *The Sun* was the 1980s. And these unsung pioneers of straight-faced news parody were a big inspiration for those of us creating *The Onion*.

Jeffrey Gurian began writing for *The Weekly World News* long after their glory years, but he carried their torch of serious comedy, delivered as the straight-man journalist. For that, his writing delighted me then as it does now.

To fully enjoy this book, imagine you're in line at the grocery store. Pretend it's 1982. Pretend there's no Internet. Jeffrey's headlines call out to you from an important-looking black-and-white newsstand packed with soap opera magazines, crossword puzzle mini-books and celebrity gossip rags. Pick it up, read it, and believe every word.

Scott Dikkers

CONTENTS

About the Author 3
Foreword by Scott Dikkers 4
Man Robs Bank with His Chin 8
Man with Infant's Head Sues for
 Discrimination. 10
College Professor Fired for Casually
 Removing His Spine in Class 12
Man Killed For Giving Girlfriend a Snail
 Instead of an Engagement Ring 14
Thin Man Travels the World
 by Overnight Mail. 15
Smithsonian Institute Proves George
 Washington Wore Wooden Pants 16
Man in Wyoming Builds Family a Nest 18
Three Thousand Pound Man Sued
 by Landlord 20
Earth Invaded by Race of Tiny Aliens 22
Baby Born with Antlers 24
Man Tattoos Muscular Body on His Own
 Scrawny Frame 25
Man Slips On Pat of Butter, Winds Up
 in Next Town 26
A Brief History of Thumb-Twiddling. 28
Man Grows Turtle Shell 30
Dentist Paints Mural on Man's Teeth
 Commits Surrealistic Dentistry. 32
Stained Glass Hats for the Holidays 34
The Whispering Village of Turkmenistan . . . 35
Bodybuilder's Bicep Explodes Killing
 Work-Out Partner 36
Doggy Dancing – A New Cure for
 Loneliness. 38
Ohio Man Literally Zips His Lip 40
High Roller Wears Moustache Made
 Out Of Gold. 42
Dentist Accidentally Extracts Man's
 Face. 44
Tap Dancing for the Criminally Insane 45
Comedian Kills Half His Elderly Audience
 with Great Joke 46

11-Foot Tall Basketball Player Found in
 Namibia Running with Giraffes 48
College Admits 10 Month Old
 Infant Genius. 50
Ex-Barber Builds Home Out of
 Human Hair. 52
Surgeon General Encourages
 Thumb-Sucking for Politicians 54
Man Stretches Out in Gym – Against
 His Will 55
Man Allergic to Clothing Gets Permission
 to Come to Work Nude 56
Short Sleeve Suits All the Rage in L.A. 58
Retired Man Teaches Cockroach
 to Dance 60
Woman with Split Personality Gets
 One-Sided Breast Augmentation 62
New Terrorist Threat – A Pants Virus 64
Hunter Lost In Wilderness Saved by His
 Moustache 65
Rent-A Beard Service Opens in Hawaii 66
Man Invents Car That Runs on Urine 68
Fairytale Town of Twenniga Baynish
 Discovered in Norway 70
Man Displays Uncanny Ability to Lift
 Heavy Objects with His Eye 72
Buffalo Company Makes Wearable
 Awnings for People 74
Man Removes Own Appendix Using
 Beer as Anesthetic 76

SHORT BITS

Brothers with Longest Police Records in
 the World Claim to be Professional
 Scapegoats 77
No More Weights – Gyms Filled With
 Furniture the Newest Craze 77
Scream Your Child to Sleep 77
Train Your Child to be Rude 77
Arabs Develop Actual Flying Carpets 78

Holding Your Own Hand to
    Avoid Loneliness. 78
Real Live Superman Foils Bank Robbery
    in Kansas 78
World's Most Dangerous Dwarf. 78
Dean of Well Known Medical School
    Mugs Student at Knifepoint 79
Congressmen Caught Towel Dancing 79
Man Robs Bank Using a Q-Tip as
    a Weapon 79
Nightlife Impresario Injured Making
    Entrance by Slingshot. 80
Man Accidentally Kills Himself Playing
    Cat's Cradle 80
Man Loses Legs to Tight Pants 80
Coming On Time – (Orgasms Cure the
    Chronically Late). 80
New Fashion Wrinkle-Underhats; Sexy
    Underwear for Your head 80
Confused Farmer Plants Cotton and Little
    Sticks, in Attempt to Grow Q-Tips 81
Throwing the Book At Him (New York
    Police to be Equipped With Objects
    to Throw at People) 81
Dentist Uses Shark Biology to Give
    People Teeth That Grow Back 81
Help Me, I'm Melting 81
Man Writes Longest Love Letter
    in History. 82
Chiropractors Advise Wearing Swim Fins
    for Back Pain. 82
Alligator Suits to Go with Alligator Shoes . . 82
Salmon Upsetting Eco System by Teaching
    Other Fish to Swim Upstream. 82
Tailor Who Tapers People 82
Women Who Massage Fruit 83
Woman Who Knits Furniture 83
Hysterical Baldness is Sweeping
    the Country 83
Beachcomber Puts Seashell to His Ear, and
    Gets Secret White House Calls 83
Woman Impregnated Through Oral Sex . . . 84
The Vikings Were Chinese. 84

Huge Turtles Used as Guard Dogs. 84
Basketball Player from China Has
    Ability to Bounce 84
Cell Phone Connection to Outer Space 85
Innocent Man Re-Headed After
    Guillotining 85
Facial Hair for Dogs 85
Speaking Polish. 86
Quill Pens Making a Comeback 86
Man Attempts to Shake Hands with
    Every Person in India. 86
Emergency Librarians Cut Down
    on Violence. 86
Face Reading 87
Allergic Archaeologist Accidentally
    Blows His Nose in Priceless Tissue 87
Sitting Bull Had to Stand 87
Overzealous Lovers Can Damage
    Partner's Nervous System. 88
Government Using Invisible Men 88
Restaurant That Serves Fumes 88
Man Dies Fish to Match His Suit 88
Deodorant Made From Manure 88
Infant Martial Artist 89
Real Estate Agent Arrested for Selling
    Small, Unusually Shaped Apartments. . . 89
Man Killed in Ironing Accident 89
Elderly Man Tours Europe on Pogo-Stick. . . 90
Retired Locksmith Covers Himself in
    Postage Stamps for World Unity 90
Pilot Attempts Trans-Atlantic Flight Using
    Only His Beard to Control the Plane 90
Contacted From Afterlife by Great
    Grandfather's Moustache 90
Dentists Unite Against the Dental Hat 91
World's Largest Foreign Sock Collection
    for Sale 91
Busiclander Discovered in Blarney Castle. . . 91
Man Robs Bank Using Piece of Paper 92
Man Crushes Head in Garbage Compactor
    and Lives 92
Farmer Discovers New Ocean Using a
    Divining Rod 92

- Book of Life Found in Israel 92
- Elderly Men's Rock Band Sweeping the U.K 92
- Man Pole-Vaults Across the Country for Charity 93
- Surgeon General Suggests Co-Workers Give Each Other Piggy-Back Rides 93
- U.N. Proposes Spelling Bee to Settle Disputes 94
- Pres. Obama Studying Ballet 94
- New Headache Remedy 94
- Vice Pres. Biden Has an Alter Ego 94
- Man Arrested for Having High Fever 94
- Elderly Women's Marathon Held in New York City 94
- Solo Ballroom Dancing 95
- Mexican Hat Dance Adopted by Sweden ... 95
- Ancient Egyptians Did Their Own Dry Cleaning 96
- Woman Convinced She's Married to a Lightbulb 96
- Schizophrenic Policeman Takes Himself into Custody 96
- Top Model Has Abdominal Organs Removed for Thinner Look 97
- Mosquito Bite Shop Opens in Philly 97
- Iraqi Police Taught to Use Jokes to Lower Crime Rate 97
- Musical Toilet Paper 97
- Obese US Citizens Donate Fat to Third World Countries 98
- Congressmen Play Hide and Seek 98
- Man Crawls Across the Ukraine 98
- Redwood Tree Grows in Couple's Apartment 99
- Feminists Insist Upon Grandmother Clocks 99
- Celebs Confer with Dead Dwarf 99
- Woman So Beautiful She Has to Travel with Paramedics 99
- Rare Virus Sweeps Japan, Victims Too Weak to Bow 99
- Screw-On Hats 99
- Club for Shy Gangsters 99
- Dentists Recommend Squeezing Food for the Elderly 100
- Man Impaled On Spike, Still Shows Up for Work on Time 100
- Trampolines for the Elderly 100
- Artificial Trees Sprout Real Fruit-Seen as Sign from God 100
- 6" Tall Tribe Found In Africa 100
- Abe Lincoln Was a Pathological Liar 101
- Socks with Heels and Laces 101
- Pitcher Throws World's Fastest Fast-Ball 101
- Igloo Collapses in Manhattan 101
- Extra-Terrestrial Race of Tiny Amphibious Beings Invading Earth through Our Toilet Bowls 101
- The Fabulous Flying Nafe Twins Take the Circus World by Storm 102
- Canadian Repair-Man Wakes Up with French Accent 102
- Ancient Cave Drawings Found of President Obama 102
- Scientists Discover Real Fountain of Youth in Brazil 102
- Speed-reader Reads 500 Books a Week 102
- Contortionist Gets Loose in White House 102
- Man Speaks Every Language in the World 103
- Woman Gives Birth to Service for 12 103
- Giant Squid Found in Man's Toilet Tentacle Meets Testicle 103
- Terrorists Hurl Themselves Across Our Border by Slingshot 103
- Man Arrested for Ordering Non-Existent Food 104
- Rare Breed of Flying Cats Discovered in Sumatra 104
- Real Life Rapunzel Charged in Prison Break 104

MAN ROBS BANK WITH HIS CHIN

EUGENE, Oregon – Career criminal Horace Pentothine literally carved himself a place in the annals of crime today, by being the only man to ever rob a bank with his chin.

Horace started out in life as a normal boy until the day his parents took him to a Thanksgiving Day parade, and he accidentally got sucked into the bell of a very large trombone.

They rushed Horace to the hospital where after three hours of surgery and metalwork he was finally removed from the trombone. The trombone was saved, but despite the best efforts of a plastic surgeon, who tried his best to repair Horace's damaged chin, he was left with a chin as sharp and pointy as a knife.

The doctor mistakenly tried convincing Horace that it was a good look for him by saying —"Don't worry Horace, you look really sharp!!!! But that was the start of Horace's deep inferiority complex.

The children in school tormented Horace because of his knife-like chin. They often stuck apples and sandwiches on it when he wasn't looking. They also used him as a barbecue skewer, and to slice up their pizza. They even invited him to the school picnic, just to use him to eat corn on the cob.

The school custodial staff did their part in making Horace feel good about himself by using him as a cleaning tool in the schoolyard.

Horace's mother did her best to make him feel useful by using his head as a kitchen utensil to chop onions and other vegetables even though it often made him cry. She thought it was the onions, but it was the humiliation of being used as a utensil that hurt him and added to his low self esteem.

Horace's father did his part by using Horace's face as an all-purpose tool, kind of like a Swiss army knife. Horace's chin also came in handy for whittling, and for electrical repairs because his father wanted him to feel useful.

In high school, Horace tried his best to act like the other kids, and actually almost attended the prom, until he accidentally ripped his date's dress, and her jugular vein, after trying his best to snuggle up to her for the photos.

Horace had been a promising violinist, but had to give that up too when he destroyed one violin after the next, piercing each one with his overly sharp chin.

Horace's inferiority complex got worse, and worse, and he developed a temper to match. People who knew him said you could actually see it in his physical appearance. He began his descent into crime and insanity, and you could tell something was very wrong just by looking at him.

He became a bad drinker, and was arrested more than once for pulling his chin on a guy during a bar fight. Anytime he heard a remark having anything at all to do with a knife, he went berserk.

This last time it happened, all the guy said to Horace was, "You're not the sharpest knife in the drawer," and that's all it took to set him off.

It was after that most recent

arrest that Horace was forced to carry his chin in a sheath.

He tried growing a beard to camouflage his chin, but it wasn't that effective. Not able to find a job, and becoming more and more anti-social, Horace was driven to a life of crime.

In his desperation, he decided to rob a bank, hoping he could use the money to reshape his chin. Once in the bank, he got the teller's attention by pounding his chin on her window, into a stack of deposit slips, piercing them easily like one of those sharp spindles they use to pierce checks in a restaurant. He passed her a note saying "I've got a chin. Fill this bag with money, or I'll use it."

Fortunately the teller had the presence of mind to press the silent alarm and within minutes Pentothine was surrounded by shotgun wielding police.

Realizing his chin was no match for their shotguns, he put it back in it's sheath, and meekly surrendered, after first claiming to have had a carry permit for his chin, which later turned out not to be the case.

Pending his trial, Pentothine has been remanded to the county jail, where they were threatening to have his chin removed if he didn't behave himself.

The warden said, "We don't allow prisoners to carry weapons in here, and this guy's chin certainly falls into that category. He's here two hours, and already tried throwing his chin at one of the guards.

And so the moral of the story is, "Never take your child to a Thanksgiving Day parade , and let him fall into the bell of a trombone, unless you want him to turn out exactly like Horace Pentothine, one of the most unusual criminals in history.

MAN WITH INFANT'S HEAD SUES FOR DISCRIMINATION

NEW YORK CITY – A major Wall Street firm is reeling from charges of discrimination after Luigi Capo D'Infante leveled a $100 million lawsuit against them, claiming he was turned down for a job as a stockbroker, because he has the head of an infant.

Capo D'Infante suffers with a rare genetic defect known as Infantilism, leaving him with the 6'1" body of a 35 year old adult man, but the head of a six month old infant.

His brain is normally developed, and he speaks in an adult voice, but he has wisps of hair, and baby teeth.

In a bizarre coincidence, Capo D'Infante claims he had no idea that his name translates to mean "head of an infant" in Italian.

According to Capo D'Infante, his trouble all started when he answered an ad in the New York Times for a stockbroker with experience, and was granted an interview.

Michael Dornlap, head of personnel at Smith Barney's Connecticut office explains, "Mr. Capo D'Infante did in fact come in for an interview, but the reason we turned him down had absolutely nothing to do with the fact that he has the head of an infant.

"The ad clearly stated 'experience needed in finance.' We needed someone to run a multi-billion dollar hedge fund. Mr. Capo D'Infante's experience with finance was handling the cash register in a bakery. He never even graduated from high school."

He went on to say that Smith Barney is very open to hiring people with disabilities, although he could not honestly say that they have any other employees with infant's heads, however he did say, "but we do have a man who limps"!

Capo D'Infante claims he was treated rudely and that they laughed at him and took pictures of his head.

The employee who actually interviewed Mr. Capo D'Infante, Noah Churn a Smith Barney employee for 30 years said, "I gave Mr. Capo D'Infante every courtesy.

"I never once mentioned his obvious disability, even when he asked me to help him untie his hat, which was a typical infant's bonnet, tied under his chin, . . . not the usual look for a major Wall Street firm!"

Churn went on to say, "We were advertising for someone with experience in underwriting IPO's, working with hedge funds, and the like. This man worked in a bakery making change for people who bought cakes and pies. "

Capo D'Infante admits he may not have been qualified for the job, but he says that Churn kept giggling during the interview , "and when he thought I wasn't looking, he took out a tiny camera and tried to take a picture of my head. That's not right."

Churn said it's customary to take photos of everyone who applies for a job for security reasons. "You're always reading about disgruntled applicants coming back seeking revenge. This way we have their photos. That's all there was to it," explained Churn.

And the only reason he laughed was because "Mr. D'infante had such a charming sense of humor!"

"If he had had the right qualifications," Churn added, "we would have given him the position, infant's head or not."

College Professor Fired For Casually Removing His Spine

WINDSOR, Ontario – As the result of a severe car accident Herb Sturm, a college professor in Windsor, Ontario, was left with a removable spine which he had to remove periodically in order to clean. When he suddenly began removing his spine at random, school officials felt they had to let him go. Now it's in the courts. This is Herb's story.

Herb Sturm had a very normal life until the unfortunate accident, where his car was crushed like an accordion. When they pulled Sturm out of his car, he was also crushed like an accordion.

Since he could not lie flat on a stretcher, they rushed him to the hospital in an accordion case.

Doctors warned him he might never walk again, or even be able to straighten up.

They tried attaching coils to his feet, and taught him to walk down stairs like a slinky.

Finally they determined that he needed a new spine, and even though it was experimental surgery at the time, Herb decided to let them go through with it. They made him a removable spine that he had to remove periodically in order to clean.

Herb felt like a new man with his new spine, and went back to teaching in the college where he had taught for so many years. Ironically his specialty was teaching Invertebrate Zoology, the study of animals with no spine.

Lately though, he had taken to casually removing his spine in class right in the middle of teaching a lesson. Suddenly, and without notice he would reach behind him, whip out his spine, and slump to the floor in a pile of clothing.

Just his face would be looking up, from the middle of this pile of clothing, and he would beg the students to help him re-insert his spine, saying things like "Please help me put my spine back in."

One terrified student explained, "Mr. Sturm tried saying it was an accident at first. "Oh look, my spine slipped out." But after the first few times, we realized he was doing it himself. He would just slump to the ground, and beg us to help him put his spine back in. That's a lot of responsibility, especially with all the nerves hanging out and all. What if it goes in wrong? Then he could blame us. It was really very scary."

Another student said, "seeing your professor casually remove his spine like that was very upsetting. It would totally disrupt the class, and made it very hard to concentrate. We were always living in fear that the next time, we would be the one who had to try and re-insert it."

A third student added, "I just can't understand why he would do something like that."

Sturm blamed his spine-removal antics on a sudden change in the curriculum, for which he said he was given no notice. He claimed that the stress of that incident caused him to remove his spine at random.

After careful deliberation, the administration felt it had no choice but to let him go. A spokesperson for the school said "We simply can not have professors removing parts of their bodies, and requesting innocent students to help re-attach them". Now it's in the courts.

Man Killed for Giving Girlfriend a Snail Instead of Engagement Ring

GILA BEND, Arizona – Hiram Trask and Emma Baldoon were high school sweethearts, and had lived together unmarried, as a couple for the last 18 years.

Each year, everyone in their town, especially Emma, expected Hiram to pop the question, but every year he had another excuse why he couldn't.

This year was supposed to be different. He had made a promise.

So when Hiram told her he had something special for her this past Valentine's Day, it wasn't unreasonable of Emma to have expected a ring.

Now she's facing life in prison because of what he actually gave her, . . . a small snail.

Valentine's Day evening, they met for a romantic dinner at Del Giorno's, the fanciest restaurant in Gila Bend.

Hiram was dressed in a tuxedo, and ordered a bottle of Gila Bend's finest, Red Rock Champagne, $74 a bottle.

Everyone assumed this was the moment they had all been waiting for.

They ate and drank their way through 5 courses, and two bottles of Red Rock, but when the dessert finally came, instead of a ring box, Hiram pulled out a little glass vial and instead of a ring, presented Emma with a small snail.

Thinking it was some kind of a joke, Baldoon tapped the snail out of the vial onto the table, and said to Hiram, "What the hell is this?"

Trask explained that he had gotten her this snail as a token of his affection. He had read about this custom in an obscure magazine, which said that in a certain tribe in the Fiji Islands, the man gave the woman he loved a small snail to prove his affection."

Enraged and embarrassed, Baldoon flicked the snail onto the floor, slightly cracking it's shell, and Hiram got hysterical.

He was screaming and crying, "My snail. Look what you did to my snail."

As he lay on the floor of the restaurant, cradling the tiny snail, Emma realized he wasn't kidding.

At that point, witnesses say, she climbed onto his back, lifted his head back by his hair, and slit his throat with a butter knife. Then she jumped up and down on the snail screaming at the top of her lungs, "Eighteen years! Eighteen years I waited for a stinkin' lousy snail."

When the police came, she didn't resist. As they took her off to jail, all she said was "I would have been happy with just a plain ring, and a couple of kids. Why did he have to bring me that snail?"

Thin Man Travels the World by Overnight Mail

HELSINKI, Finland – Travis Purn had an itch to travel. The only problem was he had no money. Did he let that stop him? Not so far.

Purn has been to 124 countries, and still has a few he intends to hit.

How does he do it? By overnight mail.

"Overnight mail is guaranteed," he said. "If something happens and I'm delayed more than a day, for some reason, they return my money. All I need to do is to get myself out of the box."

Whenever he can, he has someone waiting for him to help him break out of the mailing box.

Believe it or not, the 5'6," 110 pound Purn is so flexible he's like a contortionist.

He folds himself in half and almost flat into a reinforced box, and overnight mail's himself from country to country.

A flight to Japan that would have cost him $1200 wound up costing only $117.

The problem is in getting someone in each country to pack him up, and mail him out once he's ready to leave.

"You can only deal with people you trust," Purn says. One time I got this guy who was so drunk, for a joke, he was gonna send me to the wrong country. It's a good thing I heard him through the box, and started pounding on the sides."

Purn adds, "the key is to pack extremely light. The service is reliable, and gets me there overnight, but you really can't bring a lot with you when you're traveling this way. I just make sure I have enough water, a change of underwear, and maybe a couple of snacks, and I'm good."

He likens himself to the men who used to cross the country by riding in empty railroad cars. He refuses to refer to them as "bums," instead thinking of them as "men who knew the value of a dollar."

"Why spend $1200 bucks when you can get there for $117," he asks. "Sure it take a few hours longer, but at least I don't have any crying kids around me, and there's no guy next to me boring me to death with pictures of his grandkids.

Smithsonian Institute Proves George Washington Wore Wooden Pants

WASHINGTON, D.C. – Stories have abounded for years about George Washington's fabled wooden teeth, but it couldn't have been further from the truth. Now GNN finds out what he actually wore was wooden pants!

It has since been proven that he never had wooden teeth, they were actually animals teeth embedded in vulcanite.

However, scientists at The Smithsonian Institute in Washington, D.C. claim to have unearthed proof that the first President of our country actually wore wooden pants. Here are the facts as we discovered them.

George Washington was born at 10 o'clock in the morning, on February 22, 1732 into a dirt poor family in Westmoreland County, Virginia.

He was the first born, but later wound up with a younger sister, and three younger brothers.

George's father Augustine was chronically unemployed, and the family was so destitute that George's first diapers were made out of bark. It was all they could afford.

As he got older, the family's financial situation did not improve much, and in order to try and save some money, George's father, a talented carpenter, carved most of little George's clothing out of wood.

George's wooden pants gave him a stiff kind of walk that lasted all of his life.

As a young boy, getting ready for school in the morning, he would have to climb up on a chair, and jump into his pants. The other children made fun of him.

One of the most embarrassing moments for young George came one morning when he was late for school. As he ran into the wooden school house, his legs accidentally rubbed together, causing a spark that set fire to his school and nearly burned down the entire schoolhouse.

Some say that George never got over that, and being the laughing stock of the town actually gave him the incentive to become the first President of the United States.

Strangely enough, as much as he hated his wooden pants as a young man, he eventually grew to like them as an adult, as he found out later on that when he wore his wooden pants, he could drink as much as he wanted, and he would never fall down.

His penchant for wooden pants stayed with him throughout his entire life, and knowing that helps make sense of a couple of historical facts.

When George Washington chopped down that cherry tree, he wasn't being mischievous, as was commonly believed. He was just trying to get softer wood for his pants.

Cherry wood is acknowledged for being much softer than mahogany, which is what he had been wearing. In his earlier years, he suffered a lot from splinters in the crotch, which often put him in a bad mood, until he finally learned to sand down his pants before wearing them.

His wooden pants are actually credited with saving his life. One time his boat capsized in a storm and George was able to float comfortably on his back while his men held on to his wooden pants until help arrived.

In the famous painting of Washington crossing the Delaware, many historians had always wondered why Washington was depicted as standing up in the boat. Now we know why, . . . he was wearing his brand new wooden pants, and it's not particularly easy to sit down in wooden pants.

Man In Wyoming Builds Family A Nest

ELK MOUNTAIN, Wyoming – Wade Truesdale was proud of the house he had bought for his wife and 5 kids, until the day the furniture polishing factory where he worked closed down with no notice, and he was left without a paycheck.

With few openings for furniture polishers in the small town of 1150 people, Wade soon lost his dream house to foreclosure by the bank, and he was forced to find a new place for his family to live.

Always having been a good provider, but not knowing where to turn, he became distraught, and wandered out into the desert one day to think.

He was trying to figure out what to do when suddenly he spotted a bald eagle's nest on the ground, and it all became clear to him.

He would build his family a nest!

Bald eagles build nests up to nine feet in diameter, either in large trees, on cliffs, or even right on the ground.

Truesdale figured, "if a plain old bird can build a nest, I could certainly do a better job."

He instructed the children to begin gathering twigs, to the ridicule of the other people in his neighborhood. Even his wife thought he was nuts at first, but realized they had few options, and eventually she too began gathering twigs.

Emmaline Truesdale said, "Growing up, I never pictured myself living in a nest, but life brings you things you'd never expect. You kind of have to roll with the punches. Truth be told, living in a nest, is not as bad as I thought it would be."

The Truesdales wound up with a nest that's 30 feet in diameter, with a lovely view of Elk Mountain Lake.

It's eight feet high, for security reasons, and since as he says, "none of his children fly," they enter and leave by a special ladder Wade built to make it easier for them to come and go.

Truesdale says living in a nest has plenty of advantages. First, he says, "You never have to worry about losing your keys, like the rest of the world saddled with regular homes, with doors and locks.

"There's a tremendous sense of freedom living in a nest," he adds. "You totally feel connected to nature and to the Universe. On a clear night, you just lay back with your hands behind your head, and fall asleep just looking up at the stars.

"It's quite a spiritual experience communing with nature on that level."

As soon as he gets a job, Truesdale hopes to be able to build a second level to his nest, and has plans to put a powder room on the ground level to accommodate guests.

The only one in the family not too happy with the situation is his 16 year old son Kyle. He explains, "How am I supposed to invite girls home to visit my nest? It's really embarrassing. No girl wants to date a guy who lives in a nest."

Countering claims of nests not being safe, Truesdale said, "Are they kidding? Would a mother bird put her babies in something that wasn't safe? I highly doubt it."

Three Thousand Pound Man Sued By Landlord

SASKATOON, Saskatchewan – When Horace Bissenet moved into apartment 422 at 1335 Esterwood Avenue in Saskatoon, Saskatchewan he weighed a mere 650 pounds.

At that weight, he was still able to get around, go shopping, and basically care for himself.

Eight years later, at three thousand one hundred fifty-four pounds that is no longer the case, so when Horace had to be taken to the hospital last week for an emergency appendectomy, it wasn't that easy to get him out of his house.

Thirty men showed up to try and get Bissenet onto a loading platform. A crane was borrowed from a local construction company, and because Bissenet could no longer fit through the doorways, they had to tear down the front of the building in order to get him out.

He couldn't fit into the elevator, so make-shift ramps were placed to slide him down the steps.

He had to be secured with ropes, so he didn't slide off and accidentally crush anyone.

They weren't even able to get him into the ambulance, so they put a set of wheels onto the loading platform, attached that to the ambulance, and dragged Bissenet behind them all the way to the hospital.

Fortunately, the surgery went well, and Bissonet is expected to return home soon, but his landlord says he is no longer welcome in the building.

Tearing down the façade cost him $65,000 that he claims had to come out of his own pocket. He'd have to tear it down again in order to get Bissonet back into his apartment, and he refuses to do that.

Landlord Donald Swindell says, "I refuse to be made the bad guy in this case. The other tenants at that address have the right to have a front on their building.

"We had to take down half of the edifice just to get this guy out, and I couldn't expect them to live that way, so I fixed it. Now he wants to come back in. The man is a one man wrecking crew.

When asked about the cost being covered by his insurance, Swindell said,

"What insurance? I don't have "three thousand pound man insurance". No one expects to have a three thousand pound man living in his building. This is coming out of my pocket."

Bissenet, on the other hand claims that Swindell has been looking for an excuse to get rid of him for a long time.

"They don't call him "Swindell the Swindler" for nothing," says Bissenet. This is discrimination if I ever saw it. Just cause I'm a little overweight, he wants to take away my apartment."

Swindell's reaction was just as swift. "A little overweight? He may be a little overweight for certain jungle animals, but for a person, he's in a class by himself. People aren't supposed to be weighed in by the ton."

Bissenet says he's seen this kind of discrimination before. He belongs to a club where the members all weigh at least a thousand pounds.

Two thousand pound friends of his wanted to take an apartment together as roommates, and were turned down cold.

Swindell says, "Cases like this are changing the face of the real estate market. Years ago, you never had to inquire about anyone's weight. It would never even occur to you to do so. But it seems like more and more you're hearing stories of thousand pound men and even more, like our friend Mr. Bissonnet here.

"Landlords can't be expected to bear the brunt of housing three thousand pound men. What am I supposed to do, tear down my building every time this guy has to leave and come back? No way."

Now it's up to the courts.

EARTH INVADED BY RACE OF TINY ALIENS

GROOM LAKE, Nevada – Tiny aliens are invading Earth in starships no bigger than cigar tubes.

Recent sightings confirm that hordes of these small ships, have been spotted hovering like swarms of insects, over military and industrial installations throughout the world.

So far, four high ranking military officers, believed to be generals, are feared to have been abducted by these tiny beings, from military bases in Bad Kreuznach, Germany; Camp Henry, South Korea ; Livorno, Italy ; and Brussels, Belgium.

The only witness so far, a reputable officer, who claims to have been in the midst of a conversation with one of the generals who was snatched, described standing next to him by a window, when suddenly, "some kind of energy, like a thin beam of white light came through the glass, hit the general, and reduced him to the size of a small dot. He was barely recognizable as a man, and his uniform just lay crumbled in the spot where he had been standing."

"A moment later," he continued, "a long straw-like tube pierced the glass of the window without breaking it, and like a pipette in a chemistry lab, sucked the general, or what was left of him, up into a small cigar shaped object hovering nearby."

Undetectable by radar, and capable of traveling at speeds surpassing Voyager's record 40,000 mph, they also seem to have the capacity to become invisible. They can only be seen using a special filtered lens that NASA has developed for locating so-called "invisible" objects.

As of yet, there has been no official contact from the alien ships, and we are still not certain as to their intentions regarding the abductees, but it doesn't look good.

Unsettling reports of alien violence have been filtering in from around the world.

In one chilling incident, a German security guard who unwittingly pointed his rifle in the direction of one of the hovering craft was hit in the arm by some sort of laser-like ray that flashed from a gun-slit in one of the tiny ships.

The rifle instantly melted, and the security guard's arm was cleanly, and painlessly removed at the shoulder. One observer remarked, "there wasn't even any blood. It was as if the arm had been surgically removed, and instantaneously cauterized."

In a report still being investigated out of South Korea, an entire brigade of South Korean soldiers lost their legs below the knee, when a wide band of blinding light swept across their path. Once again, all of the wounds were bloodless, painless, and seemed to heal immediately.

Because they are the size of microbes, the numbers of invading aliens are estimated to be in the millions, if not billions.

"The hostile intent of these minute aliens is no longer in doubt," says one highly placed U.S. government source. "They seem to have only one aim – world domination."

Pilots from NORAD, (North American Aerospace Defense Command) have been mobilized, and outfitted with special goggles equipped with the special NASA lenses, enabling them to visualize the tiny ships no matter what stage of visibility they are in, however they have not been successful so far, in capturing any of them.

Scientists and space engineers from NASA, and Area 51, a secret military facility in Nevada, along with military from the 19 member countries of NATO, are said to already be deploying top secret counter-offensives around the world.

Because of their incredibly tiny size, there are rumors that our government is working on combating them with some sort of a spray, or a nuclear-powered blast of air, as opposed to bullets, or shells because as one government official put it, "How can you fire at something you can't even see?"

BABY BORN WITH ANTLERS

NOME, Alaska – Rachel Binster was expecting twins. The one thing she could never have expected was what she wound up with, . . . a baby with antlers.

She and her husband, forest ranger Bob Binster, were looking forward to the birth of their first child, and both claim they are not in the least disappointed.

Doctors had told her to expect twins, but a late stage sonogram turned up twin antlers instead.

An otherwise healthy little boy they appropriately named Rudolph, the Binsters are trying to treat him as they would any other child.

Mother Rachel says, "Ever since I was a little girl, I've always been so excited by Christmas, so I look at Rudolph as my very own little reindeer."

Dr. Alonzo Bevenitsky, a neo-natal care specialist from Anchorage was flown in to examine the child. According to Bevenitsky, "I've never seen a case of antlers before, although I did once have a child with what appeared to be a rhino's horn growing out of his forehead."

When asked about the possibility of surgical removal, Bevenitsky went on to say, "Right now, they're not attached too deeply. They're kind of small and immaturely formed as you would expect on any young moose, or caribou."

When questioned further, Bevenitsky continued, "The parents seem to like them. Personally, I would remove them now while they're still small, rather than later after they start to branch out, when the baby will feel like something is missing."

With Alaskan temperatures dipping down as low as 30 below zero, having to be dressed for cold weather is a real problem for Rudolph as far as hats go, but his Mom makes him knit hats with a big opening for his little antlers.

Dad Bob says, "When I first saw them, [the antlers] I didn't know what to think, but now I think they're kinda cute. I'll just have to be careful when Rudolph gets older, and I take him out hunting, that no one shoots at him by mistake."

Both parents have learned not to let little Rudolph get too hungry. "We can always tell when he's hungry, cause his little nose gets all red, and he shakes his head violently, often breaking things around the house."

Rachel says she can't wait until Rudolph gets old enough to buy him his first sleigh, so she can watch him pull it around the neighborhood.

Man Tattoos Muscular Body On His Own Scrawny Frame

SACRAMENTO, California – Tired of being picked on for his scrawny, toothpick-like frame, 38 year old Harold Vornado decided to finally do something about it. Six feet two inches tall, but only 118 pounds made Vornado the target of every creep on the beach. But not any more. Now they call him "Vornado the Tornado."

He didn't join a gym as most other people might, instead Vornado sought out the help of his local tattoo artist Mike "The Artist" Strunk, who tattooed the body of a weight lifter over Vornado's skeletal frame.

Strunk had made a reputation for himself in the world of body art by tattooing full size pictures of people's kids on their bodies, leading to the publication of his successful coffee table book, "Honey, I Strunk the Kids."

Actually Vornado claims to have spent years in the gym, but all to no avail. "I even got one of those all-in-one gyms for my house, but I had to fight like mad for every quarter inch I gained. Even after 11 years of strict work-outs my biceps only measured 10 inches. They were really more like "uniceps" than biceps."

Strunk said, "I looked at this like a real challenge, . . . a full body tattoo. I had heard of only one case before and that was of a 400 pound Fiji Islander who had the bodies of two 200 pounders tattooed over his own, and tried passing himself off as twins."

Vornado said due to the pain and the expense, they had to work in sections, and a couple of times they even had to stop in the middle of certain particularly difficult body parts.

"Working over the sternum is really tender," Vornado explained. There was a time for about three days when I only had one muscular pectoral muscle, and the other half of my chest was as flat as ever. But wait till they see me now."

Three months, and $6400 later, Vornado plans to take his new body to the beach this coming summer, and hopefully find the elusive girl of his dreams.

"She'll have to be comfortable with tattoos of course, but these days more women are open to that than ever before. I know one thing," he added, "These days, I'm more likely to find a woman who likes tattoos, than to find a woman who likes all skin and bones."

Man Slips On Pat Of Butter, Winds Up In Next Town

COLLINSVILLE, Illinois – When Wally Pavlicek decides to slip into the kitchen for a late night snack, he doesn't fool around.

Not only did he slip into the kitchen, … literally, … he also slipped into the Guinness Book of Records at the same time.

Pavlicek, formerly a 6'4", 600 pounder, but now a 110 pound auto parts salesman, was about to turn in for the evening when as he described it, he "had this overwhelming desire for a little something to eat."

He goes on to explain, "That was kind of unusual for me. I rarely ever eat before going to bed anymore, because since I lost all the weight I'm really pretty strict about watching my diet. My wife likes it that way."

Trying not to disturb his sleeping wife Lurlene, who now outweighs him by a couple of hundred pounds, he tiptoed into the kitchen oblivious to the fact that earlier that evening, his kids had made an art project out of little pats of butter, and left it on the floor to dry.

"I hit that first pat of butter, and flew out the window like a javelin," said Pavlicek. "It was just horrifying."

He went on to explain, "There was a wind storm brewin' that night, and it was goin' real good. The last thing I remember is flyin' down Route 159, right past The World's Largest Catsup Bottle, and the next thing I knew, I was half a mile away in the town of Mattoon, in my pajamas, stuck in the mud like a gravity knife. It was down right humiliating."

Collinsvile, a small town on the outskirts of The Windy City of Chicago is known for experiencing sudden gusts of wind up to 180 miles an hour.

Mayor Tom Wysniak likens what happened to Pavlicek to what happened to Dorothy in The Wizard Of Oz.

"Just like when Dorothy flew through the air in that tornado, Pavlicek's slight frame must have been caught in an updraft, and it carried him right into Mattoon. He's lucky he wasn't killed, or worse."

Previously the longest slip on record was set in 1918, during The Battle of the Marne, when French soldier Pierre De La Roche accidentally slipped on a banana peel and flew behind enemy lines.

That slip made De La Roche a hero. He received his country's highest honor because from where he landed, he was able to take out an important German artillery position, which helped the Allies win the war.

After 83 years, his record no longer stands thanks to Wally Pavlicek.

A Brief History of Thumb Twiddling

ADELAIDE, Australia – Most people see someone twiddling their thumbs and assume the person is just plain bored. Very few people are privy to the fascinating history behind the ancient art of thumb-twiddling, which is once again making it's mark as one of the worlds first solitary sports.

Egyptologists like Alef Bayce, Ph.D. claim that the practice goes back to the days of ancient Egypt. "In those times," he explains, "the men who desired to become High Priests were known as initiates, or adepts."

"In order for them to achieve the goal of becoming a High Priest, they had to accomplish certain tasks, among them surviving 9 days and nights locked in the Pyramids, in total darkness, with no food or water, and with only poisonous snakes for company."

Bayce went on to explain, "They also had to physically leave their bodies, and travel to the four corners of Egypt reporting on what they had seen in the course of their out-of-body experience.

Those that survived went on to become High Priests, and were given the so-called secrets of life."

Thumb-twiddling was supposedly started by these very same adepts inside of the Pyramids, who had nothing else to do for 9 days except avoid the snakes.

They said that thumb-twiddling was a spiritual experience for them, and not only centered them and calmed them down, but gave them an inner strength, and a feeling of connection to Osiris, the Egyptian god of Resurrection.

Needless to say, most of the great Pharaohs were thumb-twiddlers, as were other great men in history.

Men like Nero, the Emperor of Rome, of whom it's been said, "Nero twiddled while Rome burned," was a fervid twiddler, . . . almost to the point of obsession.

Julius Caesar was also reported to have twiddled. He claimed it helped him prepare for battle.

Many other great men, and historical figures throughout history have been accomplished twiddlers.

There had been some decline during the Middle Ages, but The Renaissance, from the 14th to the 16th century, was a fabulous time for twiddling, and many well known twiddlers made their mark.

One of the best known, Leonardo da Vinci, scientist, inventor, and artist was an inveterate twiddler, and was so compulsive about it that as early as 1503, when he first began painting the Mona Lisa, his earliest renditions actually portrayed her twiddling her thumbs.

Noted art historian Alberto Pheligma concurred, "it was only due to the influence of his patron Giuliano de'Medici, that he was convinced to remove the thumb twiddling."

Even in this country, the two things you always hear about George Washington were that he had wooden teeth, and that he twiddled his thumbs.

The wooden teeth concept has been disproved. They were actually animals teeth imbedded in vulcanite. What he did wear was wooden pants. But the thumb-twiddling was right on the money.

If you look carefully at the famous painting of Washington crossing the Delaware, . . . standing up in the boat, you'll see his hands are locked together, and he's twiddling away. He's also standing up due to the wooden pants.

Custer was a great twiddler, and actually twiddled during his last stand. Eli Whitney twiddled while inventing the cotton gin.

Napoleon twiddled while conquering land for France, although his preoccupation with twiddling was said to be what caused him to lose The Battle of Waterloo in 1815.

Renoir was a twiddler, and popularized it throughout 19th century France.

Famous explorers like Balboa and Ponce de Leon, who were often at sea for months at a time, not only were avid twiddlers, but also taught their men to twiddle. Many diaries from the time describe scenes of scores of men on deck all twiddling together.

Even some United States presidents were dedicated twiddlers, as evidenced by Ronald Reagan who twiddled throughout his entire term, as did Bill Clinton, who supposedly twiddled while he diddled. There's a claim not every twiddler could make!

These days, twiddling has once again become so popular that there are actually schools where they offer classes in thumb-twiddling.

The only downside is that twiddling has been known to be addicting, and because of that there are now also 12 step programs for people who can't stop twiddling. TTA (Thumb-Twiddlers Anonymous), currently has branches in 43 states.

So the next time you're on the subway and see some guy twiddling his thumbs, don't laugh, you may be in the presence of the next Leonardo da Vinci.

MAN GROWS TURTLE SHELL

PHOENIX, Arizona – No one was more surprised than Dave Van Nest when he went to the doctor to find out about the uncomfortable, and unsightly bump that seemed to have appeared on his back, and was told he was growing a shell.

That was more than a year ago, and despite everything doctors have tried to do, Van Nest now has a fully developed turtle shell, enveloping the entire upper half of his body.

His internist, Dr. Miles Wishpin said that he had never seen anything like that before, and was "hard-pressed" as he put it to come up with a cause for the highly unusual condition.

"We did an MRI, and a CT Scan, we tried steroid therapy thinking it was some sort of auto-immune disease, and we did every other kind of test we could think of," says the doctor. "All we could find was that the thing was really attached to him by heavy fibrous bands of tissue, just like you'd see in a turtle, and we weren't able to remove it."

Wishpin, a noted internist at Phoenix General Hospital, was forced to turn Van Nest over to the care of a local veterinarian who called in Dr. Ronaan Geshwirtz, an internationally known herpetologist he had met in veterinary school many years before.

Geshwirtz, an expert on amphibians and reptiles feels that Van Nest's problem is more likely than not genetic, although Van Nest swears that no one else in his family ever developed a turtle shell.

Van Nest, an insurance salesman has been trying to make the best of it, but it hasn't been easy.

"Clients look at me funny, and I know it's not my imagination. I used to feel I cut sort of a dashing figure," said the 6'2" Van Nest, "but none of my suits fit properly anymore, and how could I really expect them to. Armani doesn't design his jackets to cover a shell."

Van Nest credits his wife Alice, along with their three young children, with helping him to adjust to this ordeal.

"It's really not easy for them," he explained. "First of all, I'm forced to sleep on my stomach, so I try and withdraw my arms and legs into my shell when I sleep, so I don't disturb her. But every so often, I have a bad dream and roll over onto my back, and that's when the trouble starts. Out of fear, my arms and legs start to kick, and then I need her help to get back onto my stomach."

Alice adds, "living with him has become very difficult. When he rolls onto his back as he inevitably does, his little legs keep moving in the air all night, and he rocks from side to side due to the shape of his shell. We all try to pitch in to make him comfortable. The kids are still a little young yet to understand. They try and feed him little scraps of meat, covered with Calcium powder to keep his shell strong."

"The other thing they like a lot," she adds, "is that part of his physical therapy involves taking him to a nearby duck pond where he literally just floats for hours. That way they spend time with their Dad, but they also get to see the ducks."

Geshwirtz explains Van Nest's mental condition. "Psychologically, he's been through a lot. There are times he even seems clinically depressed, but unfortunately there's very little research on how amphibians and reptiles react to serotonin uptake inhibitors like Zoloft, so we're really not sure yet how to treat him."

His wife kind of summed it up by saying, "he used to be a fun, bright, outgoing kind of guy, but now there are times when I literally have to coax him out of his shell."

Dentist Paints Mural on Man's Teeth — Commits Surrealistic Dentistry

HACKENSACK, New Jersey – Besides plastic surgery, the only other medical field that has an esthetic, or artistic quality to it is dentistry. Cosmetic dentistry is one of the hottest fields around these days.

Many dentists take up art or sculpture as a hobby, because they are so talented with their hands.

Dr. Rudolph M. Pinsnay, long time cosmetic dentist, is also an artist and art collector. He's a devotee of surrealist master Salvador Dali, and has shocked the world of cosmetic dentistry by creating what he calls "Surrealistic Dentistry."

Pinsnay says too many people are bored with their teeth being white and even. He feels that many people would be happier if they had something unusual to see when they smiled, so he began working on new looks for people.

First he began on false teeth. He started out by constructing dentures with the back teeth in the front, and the front teeth in the back. "This gave many people quite a unique appearance" he said.

"When they smiled, you'd see their molars,," he explained, "and the teeth you expected to be up front were hidden towards the back. It made chewing a little more difficult, but the patients got used to it. "

Then he took it one step further. Reminiscent of Salvador Dali's famous painting "Melting Watches," Pinsnay convinced some of his patients who were looking for a really different look to consider what he called melting teeth.

He took bonding material and shaped the teeth to look like they were melting.

One patient, Herman Puniblox said, "Right after I had my melting teeth done, I went into a local diner and ordered a cup of coffee. I told the guy to make sure it was hot. Really hot. He hadn't noticed my teeth. After I drank it, I gave him a big smile, and he almost fainted. It was hysterical."

After that, Pinsnay progressed to larger more complicated works of dental art.

Ronald Biggs, a long-time patient said, "I was getting kind of tired of my perfect white smile, and so I trusted Dr. Pinsnay to create something different for me.

"He's quite an accomplished artist, and he painted a mural on my teeth, with clouds, and the ocean, and everything. He painted a sun on the roof of my mouth, and attached a little fin to my tongue so that when I open my mouth wide, it looks like a shark swimming in the water on a sunny day. It's really quite beautiful."

Pinsnay has now progressed to making plaid teeth, multicolored teeth, and even psychedelic teeth. He explains, "Some ex-hippies from the 60s asked me to make them intricately patterned teeth with psychedelic swirls. I took it one step further, and installed a black light in the tonsil region of their throats, so on a sunny day, when they smile, "it looks like a disco in there."

Stained Glass Hats for the Holidays

NEW YORK CITY – Stained glass has been used in churches and synagogues since at least 1100 A.D. but it was not until last month that it's being used for clothing.

Just in time for the holidays, internationally known hat designer Ivy Supersonic, has come out with a collection of stained glass hats guaranteed to appeal to people of all faiths, and they're sweeping the fashion world.

Stained glass has always been known for it's beauty, and for representations of Biblical scenes.

Supersonic's hats depict scenes out of the Old Testament, including Adam and Eve in the Garden of Eden, the Great Flood, the Ten Commandments, and scenes from Sodom and Gomorrah to name a few.

There are ten hats in the entire collection, and some celebs already have all ten.

The hats are different sizes and shapes, and vary from the size of a stained glass Yarmulke to a stained glass Pope's hat.

In New York City, the hats have been turning up on the club scene, where a lot of younger kids have been wearing them to all night dance parties and "Raves".

Because the hats are breakable, most come with a chin strap, and most clubs have insisted the chin straps be used for safety purposes, and to protect other patrons, aside from protecting the owner's pocketbook. The average cost of one of these works of art is approximately $1500 per glass chapeau.

Dave Edwards, manager of Trick, the hottest new club in New York says, "We love the hats, but we can't take a chance of having a dance floor filled with glass, so our security has been very busy. Now they not only have to check proof of age, and for drugs, and weapons, but they also have to check that people have their glass hats strapped on tightly while they're dancing."

Supersonic claims the hats also have Healing abilities.

"We put sort of like antennas on them that draw in the Healing energy of the Universe, and transfer it right in to the Crown Chakra, the metaphysical 7th Chakra, of Universal Love, and oneness with the Universe.

"I tend to use a lot of purple, because purple is such a Healing color," she adds.

Kids have also been seen wearing the hats during the day, where due to the sunshine reflecting through the panes, the stained glass is at it's most beautiful.

Supersonic says she has no current plans for other items of glass clothing except maybe for some "really cool sneakers with stained glass appliqués."

The Whispering Village of Turkmenistan

TURKMENISTAN – There's a tiny village in Turkmenistan called Irkhotsk where the average age is 103, and no one speaks above a whisper.

Even the town's musicians play everything sotto voce, … very quietly. Nikolai Nikolayev, 108 years old, and the mayor of the town, said through an interpreter, "Forget about yogurt, and other dairy products . All they're good for is giving you phlegm. It's whispering that is the secret to longevity."

At least that's what we at GNN thought he said. It was very hard to hear him.

People in this village have been whispering for hundreds of years.

It started about 700 years ago when the Vikings were conquering much of the surrounding area, and rumors started that they were planning on taking Irkhotsk next.

The story that circulated was that the Vikings were very light sleepers, and that they were camping out in the woods, waiting for the right moment to attack, so the villagers began whispering so as not to wake them up.

Twenty years later, the Vikings had still not attacked, and the Irkhotskians credited that to their whispering.

History has shown that the Vikings were never there to begin with, but after twenty years of whispering, it just became a habit.

Healthwise, they rival the Japanese in low rates of heart disease, and high blood pressure, but almost every Irkhotskian has a large goiter, and no one knows why.

Interestingly enough, their vocal cords have almost withered away.

There is virtually no crime, because no one argues. Nikolayev says, it wouldn't make sense. "You can't argue with anyone when you're whispering. It's not satisfying. Plus, most of the townspeople are deaf from old age."

Besides old age, the main cause of death in Irkhotsk seems to be people being run over by ox carts. They try to warn each other, but between the whispering and the deafness, Nikolayev says, "we lose two or three villagers a week."

Bodybuilder's Bicep Explodes Killing Work-Out Partner

TARZANA, California – Mike "Cannon Ball" Tortuga, Mr. Olympus for the last three years, is in shock today after having accidentally killed his best friend Dave "The Dumbbell" Donato, during a routine workout, when Tortuga's left bicep exploded, taking the top of Donato's head clean off.

Tortuga, known as "Cannon Ball" for the size of his arms, "Big Mike" for the size of his body, and "The Island of Tortuga" for the size of his ego, was formerly the proud owner of what the gym world acknowledged as the biggest arms in the world, measuring a full 32 inches when pumped.

Now he is trying to cope with the concept of being the proud owner of the man with the biggest arm in the world.

The way he tells it, "I was at least half way through with my workout. I had already been there for 3 hours, working nothing but my arms.

"I did 40 sets of Hammer Curls, 30 sets of Reverse Curls, and I was just in the middle of my 10th set of preacher curls, with 110 pound dumbbells, just the way I always do, and you know, . . . doing that little twist at the end, turning my pinky in to get that incredible peak in my biceps, when all of a sudden I heard a tremendous explosion, and that's the last thing I remember. Poor Dave. He didn't stand a chance."

Donato who was spotting him at the time, was right in the middle of yelling out "All you, all you," a common encouragement yelled out by work-out partners, to spur the other partner on to greater strength, when Tortuga's bicep exploded with the force of a land mine.

"At first we were afraid it was a terrorist attack. Unfortunately Donato was such a supportive work-out partner, he was too close to avoid the blast, . . . and he paid the price. It took his head clear off," said Manny Augusto, owner/manager of the gym. "What a mess," he added, "there was blood, brain, muscle and tendon everywhere."

Tortuga has had more than his share of bad luck this past year. Earlier in the year he was hospitalized after a bizarre accident in a club one night where he had been working as a bouncer.

He was injured when an entire group of drunken revelers accidentally leaned against his neck. They said they didn't realize it was his neck. They thought it was one of those decorative Romanesque columns.

Tortuga, who was Donato's mentor, was preparing for a pose-down to be held next month at Venice Beach in Los Angeles, and holds every title imaginable for arm development.

He's won titles for Best Biceps, Best Triceps, Best Forearms, Best Wrists, Best Palms, and Best Fingers.

Augusto said that Tortuga's arms were so big, that "you expected to see little mountain climbers trying to scale his biceps."

According to Augusto, Tortuga was one of the only men who could actually flex his index finger, which had a circumference of nearly six inches around, a true rarity in the sport of body building.

Tortuga wants to stay in the competition. He feels that once he recovers, he can get his one remaining arm up to about 36 inches, and vows not to let this incident stop him.

Augusto said, "At this point, he wants to do it for Dave. Dave would have wanted it that way."

As a matter of fact, the two men were so close that surgeons were considering an arm transplant, . . . in other words giving Donato's left arm to Tortuga, but their blood types were not compatible.

Tortuga said, "I would have been honored to have Dave's arm, even though it was only about 28" around, and I didn't really like his tattoo."

Tortuga is intending to get a prosthetic arm, and is talking to surgical supply companies about designing one with muscles, because he feels it will look strange to have one arm at 32 inches, and the other at 12. He says if he has to, he'll design his own line of muscular prosthetic limbs.

Right now, he's just trying to focus on the contest, and wondering if he'll ever find another work-out partner like "The Dumbbell."

DOGGY DANCING - A NEW CURE FOR LONELINESS

NEW YORK CITY – Leave it to New York City to come up with the idea of a dancing school for dogs, . . . not for the benefit of the dogs, but for the benefit of the people who will wind up being their dance partners. It's touted as a cure for loneliness.

"Doggy Dancing" is actually the brainchild of Dr. Dan Benzagen, Ph.D. from Columbia University, in New York City.

Dr. Benzagen explains, "people have been using pets to cure their loneliness for hundreds, even thousands of years, but never on such a deep personal level as we have been able to achieve with "Doggy Dancing."

No more having to turn down invitations to parties because you don't have a date, or a dancing partner. No more "wallflower" syndrome.

Now you can dance the night away with your dog.

Benzagen continues, "we've known for years how smart they are, and how loyal and caring they are. Of all the animals in the animal kingdom dogs may be the smartest, and most loyal, which is why you find seeing-eye dogs, and not seeing-eye anteaters, or seeing-eye ferrets.

Plus, they love the feeling of power they get by standing on their hind legs."

Dr. Benzagen said he was struck by the power of "Doggy Dancing" himself after coming home one evening after a particularly stressful day, and actually "feeling kind of down." "I turned on the radio to try and change the mood," he said, "when this jazzy kind of number came on."

"My little Shih Tsu Fong ran over, and I instinctively picked him up and began dancing around the living room with him. Within minutes, the most amazing thing happened, I forgot all about my bad mood.

I figured if it could work for me, it could work for my patients too."

You can either bring your own dog to be trained, or you can have them suggest a breed that's right for you, and buy it there on the spot, after trying it out for a few dances first, of course. That way you'll be sure you don't get a dog that would rather "sit this one out."

Canine choreographer, Terry Derenzio explains, "breeds will be chosen according to the person's physical size. Large men may choose to dance with Great Danes, small women may dance with a Collie, or small German Shepherd, according to their preference."

Because it's more effective when the dog stands on it's hind legs rather than just being held in the person's arms, certain breeds won't lend themselves to dancing quite as much, like the dachshund, the Yorkshire terrier, and the bulldog.

Other breeds seem to be natural dancers, and just seem to get into the music. "Pomeranians and Poodles love to twirl, and show off, and are good for dances where the partners don't touch, like the more modern rock and roll dances."

"For more traditional dances like the Waltz or Fox Trot," adds Derenzio, "we must rely on the larger breeds like the Doberman Pinschers, the Labradors, and the Rhodesian Ridgebacks, which surprisingly have turned out to be excellent dancers."

"Pinschers can be a little touchy, and don't do as well on a crowded dance floor, especially if someone accidentally steps on their paw. Even with training, sometimes their tempers have been known to flare."

Certain dogs also respond best to certain music. Not surprisingly, the Basset Hound seems to respond best to sad music, while the Irish Wolfhound, a natural partier, has been known to literally go wild on the dance-floor, often to the point where they have had to be physically removed.

The best part is that dogs are welcome in most places because so many people like them.

Say you get invited to a wedding and you don't have a date. Most brides really love dogs, and would probably be more than willing to let you bring a dog, especially if they knew it was going to be your dance partner.

Derenzio adds, ". . . and our dogs are trained not to go for the smorgasbord. "

OHIO MAN LITERALLY ZIPS HIS LIP

DAVENPORT, Ohio – Men have done many unusual things to try and win back women they have lost, but few have gone as far as Ned O'Reilly.

O'Reilly, who lost the affection of one Miss Irina Nemfitz, his fiancé for the last three years, was truly desperate to get her back.

She left him because as he tells it, "I couldn't help insulting her. She was always telling me to shut up, and I couldn't."

Finally, he found an oral surgeon who installed a heavy-duty zipper between his lips.

"I kept ruining our relationship with my big mouth," O'Reilly was quoted as saying.

I was very hard on Irina, and was always saying something that hurt her feelings, even though I didn't mean to. Finally she couldn't take it anymore, and she left me."

Nemfitz would only say, "I was tired of the abuse. No woman likes to be told things like "you resemble a wart with hair growing out of it," or "I've seen snakes with better legs than yours." It's bad for your confidence and self-esteem. I don't need that kind of treatment."

O'Reilly claims he suffers from a rare form of Tourette's Syndrome, where instead of blurting out obscenities, he blurts out insulting remarks.

"I know I shouldn't say them, and I try to stop myself, but I can't help it, . . . they just come out. . . . But not any more they don't. When I feel myself about to say something bad, I zip my lips together, and that's it.

Oral surgeon Dr. Sheldon Semblestein said it was the first zipper he ever installed, but feels it went quite well.

Sembelstein elaborates, "When Ned first came in, I thought he was joking. For years, women have been asking me to put in a zipper so they wouldn't eat so much. It was a standing joke, but I never really thought anyone would actually request it."

Sembelstein ordered a heavy duty zipper like the kind they use on jeans, and went to work.

"The first few days, he was a little tender, and very swollen," said the oral surgeon, "but then the steroids kicked in nicely, and the swelling went down, and the zipper eased up, and was moving nice and smoothly.

"He just has to be careful that he doesn't catch his tongue in the zipper, . . . but men are used to being careful with things like that," he laughed.

O'Reilly hoped that this drastic move would prove to Irina that he was serious about changing his behavior.

"I really love the little fat pig," he said, before he could zip up the zipper.

"It was actually Irina who gave me the idea. She was constantly telling me to "zip it". But I bet she never really thought I would do it!"

So far, Nemfitz wasn't so sure she wanted to give O' Reilly another chance. "Even if he's better in the beginning," she said, "knowing him, after a while he'll probably get lazy and start leaving his zipper open. Then what will I do?" We think that women all over understand her plight!

High Roller Wears Moustache Made of Gold

LAS VEGAS, Nevada – Lazlo "Chips" Matouche, a billionaire high roller known for betting $200,000 and even more per hand at the Baccarat tables in this gambling capital of the world, showed up at The Aladdin Hotel last week sporting a 14K gold moustache.

Matouche, an investor, made his first real money with the invention of the portable ironing board that folds up so small, you can carry it in your wallet.

Known for his extravagance, . . . he once paid more than $100,000 for a pair of rare socks supposedly belonging to Daniel Boone himself, he always seems to find a way to outdo himself.

Last year, during the Cannes Film Festival, he showed up for a Miramax party wearing a diamond encrusted beard, that he supposedly borrowed from Harry Winston Jewelers in New York.

Winston is the concern that lends fabulously expensive baubles to celebrities to wear at the Academy Awards.

Garrick Spence, the manager of the Aladdin's casino said, "When Mr. Matouche came in, the glare from the lights, bouncing off the polished gold surface of his moustache was so intense, several people around him had to wear sunglasses to shield their eyes . Frankly, we were worried that it would be a distraction for our dealers."

One of the casino's Baccarat dealers, did in fact request permission to wear "shades" while dealing cards to Matouche, who routinely flips thousand dollar chips as gratuities not only to the dealers, but to anyone standing near him when he wins, hence his nick-name "Chips."

The ornate moustache is held in place with a single gold post, like that found on an earring, which goes through a single piercing on Matouches upper lip, and is secured with a mounting that goes on the back, hidden under the lip itself, just like the little flag pins everyone seems to be wearing these days.

As a matter of fact, Matouche, originally from Hungary, but who became a U.S. citizen just last year, is such a loyal American now, he had been wearing an American Flag pin on his lip even before the events of September 11th. His spokesman said, "He is very grateful to the United States for all it has afforded him."

In a bizarre side story, one woman bystander is supposedly suing for alleged eye damage, claiming the glint from the golden moustache permanently damaged her corneas.

Matouche's lawyers, white shoe law firm, Kelly, Wyeth, McDougal, and McDougal said that Matouche is innocent, and that the truth will come out in court. They summed it up by saying, she is obviously "just trying to see what she can get" from the fabulously wealthy Matouche.

DENTIST ACCIDENTALLY EXTRACTS MAN'S FACE

BISMARCK, North Dakota – Len Wheaton went to the dentist expecting no more than a routine extraction, a procedure he had undergone many times before, . . . but this time was to be different. Very different.

Wheaton's trouble all started when he woke up one morning with his head swollen to three times it's normal size. The cause seemed to be a tooth, but he couldn't be sure.

Alone on an isolated farm, he ran down to the barn, grabbed a wrench and tried to extract what he thought was the offending tooth, which only seemed to make the problem worse.

"My hand was shakin' so bad, I had to put my head into a vise, to hold it steady, and keep it from movin' around, so as I could try and pull the darn thing," said Wheaton.

Dr. Harold Glantz was just about to leave for the day when he heard a loud commotion from his waiting room. "It was the strangest sound I ever heard," said Glantz. "Basically inhuman. I hope I never hear anything like that again. "

Wheaton had managed to drive himself to the dentist's office forty miles from his home. His head had swollen to approximately six times it's normal size by this time, and he was bellowing in pain.

Glantz took what's known as a Panorex type X-ray, a film that shows the entire head in one picture.

Upon examining the X-ray, the dentist got the shock of his professional life. "Somehow," Glantz explained, "Wheaton's head became so swollen that his face had come loose, and during the course of the extraction, he inadvertently removed the man's face as well.

In a panic, he tried to cement it back on, but it was quick setting cement, and it didn't go on straight.

Wheaton claims he now has to smile from somewhere under his chin. He also claims to have suffered intense humiliation and is suing for loss of face.

Tap Dancing for the Criminally Insane

SPOKANE, Washington – Doctors at the Spokane Home For The Criminally Insane are excited about a new mode of treatment that they feel can restore formerly insane patients to sanity.

Dr. Abraham Vyune (pronounced Vyoon), has come up with a technique using tap dancing as therapy on the most vicious, and violent criminals in order to help them change their ways.

Dr. Vyune says, "Even the most ruthless, vicious, seemingly heartless criminal can enjoy a good round of tap dancing. It seems to be good for the soul."

He began by working with Roland Bife, a man who killed and cannibalized his own parents because they wouldn't give him change for a dollar that he needed to buy some chewing gum from a machine.

Bife said, "I didn't really want to kill them. I just wanted some gum, that's all. I really love chewing gum."

Within weeks, the good doctor had Bife dancing up a storm. At the end of two months, Bife danced in a solo performance for the other inmates to the tune "The Good Ship Lollypop".

He was such a hit, the doctor was overwhelmed with requests from other inmates, ... mostly murderers and rapists, ... who also wanted to learn to tap dance.

In explanation for why tap dancing could have such an effect on people who are supposed to be so mentally ill, Vyune explains, "I can't be sure, but it seems like the rhythmic sound of the tapping, and the vibration it sets off in the body affects their brain waves in a way that calms them down."

"The powerful connection of their feet hitting the floor so rapidly somehow also seems to ground them in reality."

Of Bife's performance, Vyune said, "Bife could have been the next Bojangles if only he hadn't eaten his parents."

Bife feels he is now ready to go back out into society, and Vyune agrees, but others aren't so sure.

Just last week, one of the other inmates said that after arguing with Bife "over a lousy pack of chewing gum," Bife had snuck into his cell, and sprinkled him with seasoning while he was sleeping.

Comedian Kills Half His Elderly Audience With Great Joke

RIVERDALE, New York – All comedians like to be told they "killed" while on stage, which is a comedians way of saying they did great.

Comedian Jackie La Rue took that saying to a new level last Saturday night when he performed at a nursing home in the Riverdale section of New York, and told a joke that was so funny that half his audience passed away from laughing so hard.

There were 120 seniors in the audience ranging from 78 to 94 years old when La Rue started his act. When he finished only 62 were still breathing.

There was pandemonium in the room as emergency vehicles started pulling up outside, and paramedics came from outlying areas to try and revive the elderly people, many of whom still had smiles on their faces, even in death. Unfortunately we can't print the joke here, in case any of our readers have weak hearts.

"We wouldn't want to be responsible for any more deaths from this joke," said Derrick Clontz, Editor-In Chief, of a major New York publication. We just don't have the insurance to take a chance and print it."

He added, "We will tell you it had to do with farmers, a sardine, a stripper, and a compass. Any more than that, and you might be able to guess it for yourself."

La Rue took it very hard, and may retire after this comedic tragedy.

He spoke with GNN and said. "It wasn't even one of my funniest jokes. I have stronger stuff than that, but I held back."

Many of the relatives have already contacted lawyers with regard to filing suit against the comic for massacring so many of the elderly residents of the home.

One woman who lost her 89 year old mother said, "There was just no reason for him to have to have been that funny. If he had been just a little less funny, my mother would still be alive today."

As a result of this tragedy, Congressman Bradley Newton (D) from New York has proposed legislation to actually outlaw comedians from being too funny with people over a certain age.

Comedy clubs usually serve alcohol, and are used to checking proof to make sure their audience is of a legal age to drink.

Now bouncers would have to check not only age, but also medical histories, and comedians would be rated as to how dangerous their material could be to people with heart conditions or high blood pressure.

La Rue said, "I was only trying to entertain the old people. I didn't want to hurt anyone."

11' Tall Basketball Player Found In Namibia Running With Giraffes

INDIANAPOLIS – At 7'7", Manute Bol never thought he'd have to look up to anyone in his life, but next to 20 year old, 11' tall Ohno Imbabwe, from Namibia, Bol looks like an infant.

When NBA scout Bud Parker was on safari in Namibia, he saw what he thought was a group of giraffes frolicking at a watering hole in a jungle clearing, but he had to take out his binoculars to verify what he saw next.

At first he thought it was a giraffe with a human head, but it turned out to be a man who was so tall, he actually played with full grown giraffes, and handed them leaves from their favorite acacia, mimosa, and apricot trees.

Although Namibia has one of the lowest population densities in Africa, it is still home to several unusual tribes.

The Gotinka Tribe members average 7 to 8 ½ feet in height, generally acknowledged as the tallest people in the world.

At 11' tall, Ohno is considered tall even for them, and is basically accepted as the tallest man not only in the tribe, but in that part of Africa.

His mother Ontebbe is 7'8", and his father Gorunda is 8'4", but Ohno towers over everyone, and because they were so poor, and he had no toys, he grew up playing with giraffes.

Female giraffes may be 14-15 feet tall, and males can be as much as 15-17 feet tall.

They range in weight from 1210-3960 pounds, and Ohno would run with them as they reached speeds of up to 35 miles an hour.

For some reason, they seem to have accepted him.

Parker offers a guess that "maybe because of his extreme height, they may have thought he was a small giraffe himself."

Like the giraffes, Ohno has learned to sleep standing up, and as big as he is, he's still fast and agile.

Parker convinced Ohno's parents to let him bring him to America, which he did three months ago, all expenses paid.

In order to even get him on a basketball court, they first had to make him custom made sneakers to fit his size 32 EEE feet.

At 540 pounds of muscle and sinew, there is basically no fat on his body.

For breakfast, he can eat 2-3 dozen eggs, with two loaves of bread, and doesn't gain an ounce.

He seems to be taking to the sport rather well so far, and amazingly has to actually bend over to dunk the ball, as the rim of the basket is only 10 feet off the ground.

If Imbabwe jumps, he stands more of a chance of missing the basket than if he stays firmly planted on the ground.

Parker managed to get him a scholarship to Indiana State University, where they're grooming him to be a power forward.

His dormitory room is equipped with two king-size beds attached together head to toe to accommodate his immense size.

He has also been working with a tutor to teach him English ever since he arrived, and is doing quite well.

Imbabwe has already made quite a name for himself, and intimidates every team he comes up against.

Jesse Crouter, head coach of Indiana State said, "not only does he block the other players, he blocks out the sun. When Imbabwe comes out on the court, it literally looks like an eclipse."

One of his teammates added, "When the opposing team sees him coming, they usually wind up saying, "Oh no, it's Ohno."

College Admits 10-Month-Old Infant Genius

FRANKFORT, Kentucky – Most 10-month-old babies are still pre-occupied with cutting new teeth, and trying to take a few steps, but little Wiley Marshall has more important things to do, like preparing for an organic chemistry exam, and completing a paper on Global Warming for his Earth Science class.

Wiley is by far the youngest student ever admitted to Kentucky State University, and so far he seems to be holding his own.

Born with the ability to speak fluently, in grammatically perfect adult-type English, he reportedly greeted both his Mom and Dad in the delivery room to the utter shock of all those in attendance.

The doctor slapped him on his fanny, and he reportedly yelled out, "Hey Doc, not so hard. I'm just a baby."

Then he went on to thank his Mom and Dad for giving birth to him.

Dr. Ronald Winters, the attending Ob-Gyn. Specialist, who delivered Wiley at Maimonides Children's Hospital, was quoted as saying, "I thought the child's father was an amateur ventriloquist or something, and was throwing his voice to have some fun with me, until I saw the baby's lips moving. I've never seen anything like it in my life. "

By two months old, Wiley was already reading the local newspaper, although he needed a little help in holding it.

At 4-months old, he composed an op-ed piece his mother helped him write, that got printed in the paper, on the inequities that infants face in our society.

"People treat us like babies," he said angrily.

At six months of age, he was walking pretty well, and was able to write clearly on his own. He took the admissions exam for Kentucky State University the same month, and passed.

According to Wiley, the personal interview was the most difficult. "I couldn't see well from the seat where they put me," he explained, "so I had to ask to be put right up on the conference table."

Needless to say, he was accepted.

The normal size for a 10-month old infant, Wiley sits in class in a specially designed seat that straps him into place, and his teachers swear they don't mind having to stop the class every so often to change him, or give him his bottle.

Ursula Baysche, head of the math department says, "Obviously Wiley is a gifted student, and the opportunity to work with someone so special is worth the small inconveniences of having to clean up after him when he "cheeses," or suddenly begins crying for no reason. It doesn't happen often. "

Socially, he's kind of a loner, and seems to prefer staying by himself in his room after class rather than hanging out with his classmates.

One of them, a young woman who prefers to remain anonymous says, "We invite him to come out with us, to try and make him feel more comfortable, and one of the crowd, but he always turns us down."

Obviously Wiley looks too young to get into the bars where all the kids on campus hang out.

She adds, "Even with proof, the bouncers would still hassle him."

The Marshall's have two other children 6, and 8 who often ask their baby brother to help them with their homework.

Wiley's mom Emma seems to be taking all this all in stride. "People always say it's so frustrating having an infant, 'cause you never know what they want," she said.

"With Wiley, there's no doubt what he wants. He never shuts up. He definitely takes after his father."

EX-BARBER BUILDS HOME OUT OF HUMAN HAIR

SVENSPOT, Sweden – Most people work all their lives to be able to afford the home of their dreams, but Oslo Thorgensson's dream was a little different than most.

Thorgennson spent most of his adult life as a barber in his native town of Svenspot, Sweden.

Fascinated by hair since he was a small child, he kept every single hair he ever cut from every single customer he ever had, over his 40 odd years in business.

He kept the hair in bales, in a separate storage house, like some farmers keep hay in a silo.

Last year he retired to build the home of his dreams, an entire home made from human hair.

It took him almost two years to build.

He wove the hair together, shaped it, styled it, and sprayed it into the home of his dreams.

When questioned about the strength of the whole thing, he explained.

"Hair is a lot stronger than most people give it credit for. The hair that holds my door in place is tightly knotted, and in other areas where strength was important, I even braided the hair, if I felt it was necessary."

He went on to elaborate that "anyone who ever got a knot in their hair knows it's almost impossible to get it out without cutting it out."

The only rules in his house are no smoking, and no gum chewing, and if you've ever gotten gum stuck in your hair, you already understand why.

Washing his hair home can be problematic, but he uses a special shampoo that he developed that is fast drying, and doesn't cause split ends.

Thorgensson says, "On a sunny day, … and in Sweden our sun is very strong, … you can look at the shape, or the outline of the house, and you won't see any split ends sticking out, like you do when you look at some women's hair in the sun. My house has the healthiest hair in the neighborhood," he says proudly.

The most interesting part to some people is the assortment of colors. The front of the house is blonde, while the rear is brunette.

The sides are brown and black, with little flecks of gray, and the roof is red.

Thorgensson said he always favored red, and "it's the easiest to take care of, and the most manageable, which makes it perfect for the roof."

He claims he's never bored, and loves just lying back, and looking up at all the hair he's accumulated.

A far as problems are concerned, he claims that his biggest problem is wind, because it often changes the shape of the house, and he has to hold some of the hair in place with clips, in order to keep it from looking windblown.

He has hair curtains over the windows, which kind of gives the effect of someone having their hair hanging in their eyes. "You almost want to brush it back sometimes," he says.

Not everyone is particularly thrilled with Thorgensson and his house of hair. The neighbors are threatening to sue for ruining their property values.

Olaf Turngren for one says he hopes his neighbor's house goes bald for what it's done to the neighborhood.

"First of all," he says, "sightseers come at all hours of the day and night. The man is stark raving mad, and no one reputable will want to live here anymore. It's a shame."

And Thorgensson's wife Rebecca left him after being married for thirty years, because of his hair house. When contacted by WWN she would only say, "I put up with a lot over the years, but if he thought I was gonna lay down with him on a bed of hair every night, he was sadly mistaken. This hair fetish of his has gotten completely out of control."

The only problems he admits to are that birds build nests in his roof, and once, he claims his living room developed a bad case of dandruff, but that's it.

Thorgensson seems to be living his dream, and no matter what the weather, on hot summer days, or cold winter days, he can usually be found outside, brushing his house.

Surgeon General Encourages Thumb-Sucking For Politicians

WASHINGTON, D.C. – Dr. David Stamen, Acting Surgeon General has come out with a new report actually encouraging politicians to suck their thumbs in public.

Babies suck their thumbs to gain a sense of security, and Dr. Stamen feels that many politicians, especially those entrusted with the public welfare, go through periods of deep insecurity, especially in times of national trouble.

He feels that sucking their thumbs would give them the clarity, and security they need to make those big decisions, and stay level-headed, especially in times of crisis.

Dr. Walter Bimm, head of Psychiatry at Capital City Hospital agrees. "As outlandish as this may sound," he says, "we've known for a long time that all people begin life with an oral fixation, because that is the first way we relate to the outside world, ... with our mouths.

"Either through mother's milk, or by drinking from a bottle," he added, "we learn to feel secure by experiencing a sucking sensation. The problem is that we think just because we grow up physically, we no longer have those feelings of insecurity. That couldn't be further from the truth."

The reason for the study is that they're afraid that the personal problems of many of the members of Congress are starting to leak over into their job performance, affecting their ability to make decisions.

As a result of the Surgeon General's report, several Senators and Congressmen have already started sucking their thumbs, and are giving this theory a try. They seem to have varying opinions.

Rep. Niles Turmley, (D) from West Virginia says, "At first, it felt a little awkward sucking my thumb in Congress, just before a big vote, but then I realized that I owed it to my country to try this.

If the Surgeon General says it will help me feel secure, and make better decisions, then that's the least I can do, . . . and you know what? It's not half bad."

However, Rep. Randall Quist,(R) from Kansas says, "I feel like a damn fool sucking my thumb in front of all those other guys. I did it because I'm a patriot, and because I felt like I owed it to my country to try it, but to be honest with you, I don't like it one bit."

"I believe in serving my country, but you have to draw the line somewhere. Next thing you know, they'll be telling us to wear diapers!"

Man Stretches Out In Gym – Against His Will

CHARLESTON, West Virginia – Ralph Swane went to his gym expecting to get stretched out, but he got a lot more stretching than he bargained for.

Swane had been working out with personal trainer Rick Graden for the last few months, and Graden had been starting each work-out with vigorous stretching, but this last one seemed to go way beyond that.

Swane describes being strapped onto a machine similar to a rack used in The Middle Ages to torture prisoners, with metal cuffs on his arms and legs, while Graden slowly turned a wheel that stretched and elongated Swane's entire body.

Swane claims he heard his joints popping, and that he screamed for Graden to stop, but Graden encouraged him to "try and go beyond the pain."

"He just kept telling me 'no pain, no gain, . . . no pain, no gain', and I was embarrassed to continue screaming because of all the pretty girls working our around me, so I just bit down on the ball and leather strap he put in my mouth."

Graden's account is much different. "He really seemed to enjoy the stretching on our new "Torquemada Stretch Machine," because he was always complaining that he never had enough flexibility. He has much more flexibility now, so I don't know what he's complaining about."

Swane continued, "After the stretching, I felt too weak to actually work out, so I went back to my locker to get dressed, and none of my clothing fit."

"I went to put on my pants, and they were like highwater pants, about 6 inches too short. My shirt was so short, it exposed my whole midriff. I felt like Brittany Spears. I thought I had somebody else's clothing on."

Swane said the added benefit of growing 6 inches, and going from 5'7" to 6' 1" so rapidly is eclipsed by the elongated shape of his body.

"It just doesn't look natural" he said. "I look like a tube of toothpaste that was squeezed in the middle instead of at the bottom. I have a very strange shape now. "

Swane may not like it, but the head of the University of West Virginia Medical School's growth and development department is interested in talking to Graden about joining their staff to aid them in their studies on increasing growth in adults.

Man Allergic to Clothing Gets Permission to Come to Work Nude

PENSACOLA, Florida – Jack Navish had worn clothing all his life, and never had a problem, until the day he came down with an unexplained full body rash. Now he goes to work totally nude.

At first, he assumed the rash was from a new detergent, or maybe a reaction to some food he ate, but day after day went by, and instead of getting better, it continued to get worse.

His doctor prescribed a dose of Benadryl, 50 mg. every four hours, but it did absolutely nothing.

They proceeded to try every steroid cream and lotion on the market, and consulted every dermatologist within a 100 mile radius of his home, all to no avail.

It finally became uncomfortable enough that when he got home, he had to take off all of his clothes, and walk around in the nude.

Almost immediately upon doing that, Navish began noticing a change, but as soon as he got dressed the next morning, the rash continued to itch and get worse.

After finally seeking help at an allergist's office, where literally hundreds of tests were done, he was given the terrible truth that he was indeed allergic to clothing.

Dr. Salman E. Trafe, head allergist at Ockalocka State Hospital says, "I've seen people allergic to certain fabrics before, like wool or silk, but never in my 30 years of practice have I ever seen a man become allergic to all articles of clothing, no matter what they're made of.

If I hadn't seen it with my own eyes, I wouldn't have believed it."

For the past 26 years, Navish, 48, has worked as a lawyer and partner at the white shoe firm of Skavey, Phelps, and Windham, one of the biggest law firms in Florida.

He was in charge of bringing in new business, and meeting with new clients,

It was hard enough explaining to potential clients why, thanks to the warm weather in Florida, he had started coming to work in the briefest of T-shirts and shorts, leaving as much of his body exposed as possible.

But, when even the briefest Speedo, and cut off shirt became too much, Navish had no choice but to request that he be allowed to come to work nude.

"I was really afraid that a request like that might cost me my job, "he said, "but I basically had no other choice."

After much debate among the other partners, mostly because of his 26 year history with the firm, they voted to allow him to come to work naked, but only if he kept it low key, and didn't disturb either the other employees, or negatively impact potential clients.

One new client, Suzie Whitcolm of Whitcolm Enterprises says, "In all honesty, when I first came to meet Mr. Navish, I thought his nudity was a little odd. But after the first few minutes of hearing his presentation, I realized that he had such good ideas for my company that I was able to get past the awkwardness of his nudity, and really began to listen. Now, in retrospect, I'm glad I stayed."

In an unusual update on this story, a local artist named Cheyenne may have come to Navish's rescue by offering to use bodypaint, and paint pants, and a shirt and tie onto Navish's naked frame, much more in keeping with the law firm's previously conservative staid image.

One astonished law partner commented, "Jack's a good man, but paint or no paint, it's obvious that the man is naked. It's starting to sound a little like The Emperor's New Clothes around here!"

Short Sleeve Suits All The Rage In L.A.

MILAN, Italy – Internationally known and respected men's clothing designer Fabrizio Bellantonio, has managed to shock the usually unshockable world of men's fashion by designing what he calls the perfect combination of business style and work-out/physical fitness ethic, . . . the short sleeve suit.

Now you can attend that important business meeting but still impress the girls with your well developed biceps.

Made to be worn with short sleeve shirts and French cuffs, the cufflink usually sits in the center of the bicep, really showing off the muscle to it's best advantage, especially when reaching across the conference table to pass that heavy water pitcher, raising your hand to make that salient point, or "casually" lifting your heavy briefcase filled to the brim with earth-shaking, innovative ideas.

Cuff sizes are adjustable according to the size of the bicep, and some gyms are already putting out their own short sleeve suits to accommodate the huge number of bodybuilders who still like to dress up, but are often unable to find suits to accommodate their huge arms, without spending a fortune on custom made suits.

Most suits come with an extra pair of pants like they did in the 1930s, when it was commonplace for most fine suits to come with two pairs of pants.

One pair are long, the other pair are cut like shorts to allow the men to show off their calf muscles, and quads as well.

With physical fitness on everyone's mind, and people feeling so much more proud of their bodies than they have in the past, many men have felt they were not able to show off all their hard work in the gym while wearing a regular suit.

This feeling has been proven beyond a shadow of a doubt to have adversely affected productivity in the workplace.

Dr. Salman Shnayvid of The University of California at Encino, noted research scientist in the field of sociology, states, "Men who are happy with their bodies and who take pride in showing them off, tend to do much better work, and get more things accomplished during the course of an average day at the office.

"These short sleeve suits allow them to do a good days work, and still feel good about themselves."

The women in the office seem to like them too. Margaret Wallace, head of productivity research at I.C.G., one of the biggest tech firms in the nation, claims that these short sleeve suits increase women's productivity as well. According to Wallace, "A man with good arms in a short sleeve suit is like a shot of adrenaline to many women, who after working hard all day, can certainly use a visual treat."

The suits are flying off the racks, and are being sold at only the best stores. A Bellantonio suit usually starts at $1200 and goes up from there. One customer, a little lighter in the pocket after buying three of the suits said, "You have to pay an arm and a leg for these exciting new creations, but sometimes that's what it takes to stay stylish and well-dressed."

"Also," he continued, "what better incentive to keep going to the gym? They just don't look as good when worn by guys with pipestem arms." With the advent of the short sleeve suit, now men can be considered well dressed, and casually dressed at the same time.

RETIRED MAN TEACHES COCKROACH TO DANCE

NEW YORK CITY – Harold Robison spends most of his days in a dingy, roach infested room of The Skylight Hotel, an SRO on the West side of Manhattan. Retired for many years, he claims to have once had a spoon repair business that went bust with the advent of plastic, disposable silverware, and that he was never able to get anything else started.

He has few amenities except for an old 8 track tape player from the early disco days, and a 12" black and white TV.

A loner with no real friends, most of his days were taken up with trying to figure out ways to kill the roaches that infested every inch of his apartment.

No matter what Robison did, he couldn't seem to get rid of the roaches.

It's estimated that roaches have been around for some 280 million years, and are known as the ultimate survivors.

After a few months of trying every thing he could think of, in spite of himself, he actually wound up admiring them for their tenacity.

In effect he decided if you can't beat them, join them.

He decided to try and get to know them, and instead of killing them, began feeding them, and eventually began making them little outfits.

He began to notice that when they heard certain music, their little antennas started to wiggle in time to the music.

"The faster the music, the faster they would wiggle," he said. "On a really fast song, some would wiggle so fast, they'd flip over with their little legs going like they were on a bicycle."

Robison wondered if he could teach them to dance. He went and got books on roaches, and read that for many years scientists had hypothesized that if any insects could dance, it would be the roach.

They had six legs, with 18 knees, . . . plenty of room for flexibility, plus they can hold their breath for up to 40 minutes, so they wouldn't get winded from strenuous dancing.

Robison chose one particular roach to start with, and named him Max, (no relation to the jazz drummer!)

He claims that when Max hears disco music, he gets up on his tail end and dances.

Dr. Maxwell Punitz, head of entomology at N.Y.U.'s biology department was skeptical about the dancing roach until he actually went over to Robison's hotel to see for himself.

"I had to go and see it with my own eyes. I wasn't happy that he called the roach Max, but I must admit, he was definitely dancing.

The strangest part about it was that his favorite song to dance to seemed to be that old Gloria Gaynor hit, "I Will Survive."

Woman with Split Personality Gets One-Sided Breast Augmentation

RALEIGH, North Carolina – Many people have been known to have split personalities, but not right down the middle!

Heidi Snackle of Willardsville, North Carolina holds the dubious distinction of having a split personality, that literally split her in half, with two opposing personalities, and now she's got one very large breast to show for it.

Her right half is an incredibly sexy woman, with a bad reputation, while her left half is a virgin, very conservative, and demure.

Her right side wears make-up, and dresses real flashy, while her left side wears no make-up, and basically dresses like an old maid.

Her right leg is exposed with a short leather mini-skirt, a fishnet stocking, and a boot.

Her left leg on the other hand, can not be seen as it is hidden by a floor length dirndl dress, with a plain back shoe, and a woolen stocking.

The right half gets drunk, and carries on with men, while the left half looks on horrified.

Each personality speaks out of a different side of her mouth, so there were times when she would argue with herself, rapidly contorting her mouth from one side to the other, increasing in speed as the argument intensified.

The problems also intensified when the right side decided on getting breast augmentation, but the left side wouldn't hear of it.

The right side said she wanted it for the summer months on the beach, when the right side wears a bikini, and the left side wears an old skirt-type bathing suit.

Dr. Walter Midroff, head plastic surgeon at Raleigh Memorial explains what happened next.

"Ms. Snackle appeared at my

office seeming very confused. The right side of her mouth requested a breast augmentation, while the left side of her mouth fought against it. I felt like King Solomon for a minute. I was able to settle the matter by suggesting that she only do one side, and fortunately that seemed to satisfy both sides of her mouth."

Dr. Midroff went on to say, "Being that she was only doing one side, I tried to convince her not to go larger than a C, as she had only been an A when we started. The right side of her mouth insisted on a D cup, and wouldn't hear of anything less. I had no choice but to do what the patient requested. I had her sign a release, and that was it."

Now that she's had the surgery, she's been seen around town wearing half of a low cut dress on her right side, and a high necked dress on her left.

She says she's perfectly comfortable with the results, and just wishes her left side would come around to her way of thinking, and "go out and have some fun for a change."

New Terrorist Threat – A Pants Virus

ALBUQUERQUE, New Mexico – In an unusual move, without disclosing the source, the government has announced the discovery of secret captured documents, detailing a plot to unleash a dreaded pants virus in this country.

Not naming the terrorist country, except to say they don't dress the same as we do, this avowed enemy of The United States, appears to have developed a virus so specific that it only attacks men's pants.

The rationale seems to be that they realize they can't beat us militarily, so they're trying to humiliate us in the eyes of the world by destroying every pair of pants in the country, leaving us a nation of men in our underwear.

In an unusual twist, women's pants don't seem to be at risk.

The cause for that can't be chivalrous, because women are treated like third class citizens in that country anyway.

It's just that they know that American women like to show off their bodies, and wouldn't particularly be threatened by the loss of their pants.

Men on the other hand have very fragile egos, so it's just our men that they want to humiliate.

Picture President Obama having to make a speech in his underwear. That's their goal.

Even worse, he might have to wear women's pants, until more men's pants can be made.

To counteract this threat, the government is asking manufacturers in the pants business to step up production, so we can store away at least three pairs of pants for every man in the country.

Five star general Bill O'Donohue says, "We'd hate to have to dip into our pants reserves, so we're asking all the manufacturers to step up to the plate, and do the right thing."

In the past, our pants reserves have been limited to only one pair for every man in the country.

The new emergency pants will be stored underground, in special virus proof containers, keeping them safe in case this pants virus attack comes to fruition.

Scientists have a preliminary version of a protective spray that men can use to protect their pants from the virus.

The only problem seems to be that no matter what color the pants are, it turns them a bright orange.

Dem. Senator Hugh Porcine of Alabama says, "Many men might not want to be seen in bright orange pants. Aside from not matching most other clothes, they look like prison jumpsuits."

As a comedic aside, he added, "Come to think of it, that might be just right for some of our politicians."

Hunter Lost In Wilderness Saved By His Moustache

NOME, Alaska – Axle Hunter, who true to his name, is an actual hunter, was reunited with his family today after being lost in the Alaskan wilderness for six long days and nights while hunting for caribou.

He thought he would never find his way out again, until he realized he was able to use his moustache as a compass.

He knew the territory like the back of his hand, but an accidental fall caused him to hit his head, and he was knocked unconscious. When he came to, he had no idea where he was.

Hunter, the proud owner of a thick Salvador Dali type moustache, with the ends majestically turned up towards his eyes, had always found solace in stroking the ends of his moustache when trying to solve a serious problem.

Being lost in the wilderness for six days definitely fell into that category. With all of his food gone, and freezing to death, he certainly thought he was a goner.

With the faces of all 16 of his children flashing in front of him, he was determined to solve his dilemma. As he always did in tense situations like that, he went to stroke his moustache, and found one of the ends turned out in a different direction than it was supposed to be.

Automatically assuming it was because of the cold, he tried twisting it back into place, only to find it turned out again by itself, as if his moustache somehow had a mind of it's own.

After wrestling with his moustache for a few moments, he realized that maybe it was trying to tell him something.

One end seemed to be pointing straight out from his face, while the other end was pointing completely in the opposite direction.

Laszlo Purnabule, a local scientist, offered a possible explanation for this phenomenon by explaining that hair carries static electricity.

"For some miraculous reason," Purnabule hypothesized, "the hair of Hunter's moustache stored up that electricity, and became magnetized like a compass."

Hunter was able to figure out that the left side of his moustache was pointing North, while the right side was pointing South.

He himself described it as being "absolutely amazing."

Slowly but surely he made his way back to civilization. Every time he made a wrong turn his moustache would spin "like a propeller" as it guided him on his way out of the wilderness.

His wife Eloise said, "I always hated that moustache. I used to beg him to shave it off. Who ever thought it would wind up saving his life?"

RENT-A-BEARD SERVICE OPENS IN HAWAII

HONOLULU, Hawaii – Most men take it for granted that they can grow a beard any time they want, but that's not the case for everyone.

Statistics say that one out of every seven men can not grow a beard, or if it does grow in, it grows in sparsely like a billy goat.

One out of seven is about 15%, and much higher than most people would think.

There seem to be many more follically challenged men out there than previously believed, and for many of them it's genetic.

There are many men in both the Asian, Hawaiian, and Native American communities, as well as many plain ordinary Caucasian American men who are follically challenged in the facial area.

They would love to go around sporting a beard, but it just doesn't grow. Now, thanks to a man named Abe Tahanaka there's a solution.

Mr. Tahanaka is part Japanese, and part Orthodox Jew.

The Orthodox Jewish part of his family is used to having long, full flowing beards. Many men on the Japanese side of the family can only look on in envy.

While some Japanese men can grow beards, they're often of the long, thin variety, stereo-typed in many U.S. movies of the 1940s and 50s.

Mr. Tahanaka has simply seen a need and filled it. He created Rent-A-Beard, and it's taken off like wildfire.

His new catalogue, featuring some of the top male models in the industry, is amazingly exciting, and packed with different styles.

Now every man can have the beard of his dreams, including custom made, monogrammed models, so when you send them to the cleaners, you're sure to get your own beard back.

He has all length and all color beards. He even has a reversible beard for men who need to pack light when going away, but know they'd like a change of beard when they reach their destination.

He has an entire line of winter beards for men traveling to places where it snows.

For skiers, there's a beard that even comes with a detachable hood, and another model without the hood, that comes slit up the middle, and doubles as a scarf.

Or you can get the battery operated heated model that actually swings like a pendulum, while keeping you warm, and stylish looking.

Renting a beard has become so popular, that most clubs and restaurants are having to open beard check rooms.

Many men seem to prefer checking their beards before they eat, only to reclaim them before the dancing and festivities begin.

Any time something catches on so big, you can be sure that one way or another, crime will manage to infiltrate, so Abe also offers the very newest thing in beard security, a beard with a homing device, guaranteed to stop the increase in beard-jacking.

Abe says, "Picture this scenario. Two guys come up to you with guns drawn. You know they're after your beard. Now you can give them that beard, and not have to worry that you'll never see it again. Let them get safely away, press a little remote button, which activates a homing device, and the police will have you and your beard reunited before your face even knows that it's gone. "

The very newest and most expensive model is a battery operated heated beard, as opposed to the old kind that you had to plug in, so you can feel comfortable walking into that hip party knowing that your beard can swing like a pendulum for hours, without having to stay close to an electrical socket.

Beards can either be rented or leased. Discounts are offered on volume purchases.

Man Invents Car That Runs On Urine

MONTAIGNE, Switzerland – Tired of the frustration of Western nations being held hostage by countries that hate us, but still having to deal with them because we need their oil, inventor Jacques Flaubert has stunned the automotive world by inventing a car that runs on something we all have access to, . . . urine. He calls it "The P-P Car."

Scientists have been searching for an alternative fuel for many years, and now Flaubert seems to have come up with it, . . . common, everyday urine. Flaubert has invented many things in his life. Among his best known inventions were leather socks with heels, and laces, and a plastic chin holder on a stand, for students with narcolepsy who fall asleep uncontrollably in class.

"The stand attaches to their desk with a vise-like clamp. They put their chin in the holder, and it keeps their head from falling forward, and embarrassing them, when they inevitably fall asleep," he explains.

Flaubert's previous inventions were for a small select group, but his urine car could potentially revolutionize the entire world.

"The Western world is always bemoaning it's reliance on Middle East oil," he explained, "and even though gasoline has always been expensive in Europe, Americans especially are tired of paying close to five dollars a gallon for gasoline. Now they can have all the fuel they want, . . . for free."

"They won't have to be worried about possible gas restrictions like what happened in the 1970s. They will never again have to line up at gas stations for fuel. Now there will be urine stations, with urine pumps."

Where people used to stop off at gas stations to use their bathrooms, now those very same bathrooms can be used to fill the pumps.

"People don't realize the value, and chemical content of urine," he says. "Most people take their urine for granted, but every single day, in every country that has plumbing, they p _ _ _ away tons of valuable fuel."

Flaubert, a biochemist, goes on to explain, "there are approximately 200 known biochemical compounds in urine, and some scientists believe there may be as many as thousands.

"Once the urine is filtered through the kidneys, the toxic matter is filtered out," he explains, "and it makes a clean burning fuel."

"Refueling your car may pose certain problems in the beginning, as breast feeding does for some women who are not sure just where it's appropriate to do it.

"Out of pure modesty, some men may want to pull over to the side of the road before entering the tank."

In terms of ease, "It would certainly be a lot easier for men than for women," admits Flaubert, "as men come with their own hose," so to speak.

However, women will be afforded the luxury of "filling up" from inside the car."

Women would use a funnel system that could be hooked up to open directly under their seat so they could use it when driving alone, and they wouldn't even have to pull over. "

The driver's seat would in effect be like a leather toilet seat, that would open and close by way of a switch.

Flaubert figures his urine car will get about 20 miles to the gallon of urine. The trunk will have a special storage area that can hold several bottles of water, which will feed into a holder in the glove compartment on a conveyor belt, as each successive bottle of water is used.

That will help prevent anyone from ever running out of fuel. "All you need to do is to keep drinking," says Flaubert," and you can keep producing more fuel as you drive. "

Men with prostate conditions will be able to call for emergency on-road service in the event they can not fill their own tanks, but on-road service groups like the AAA are up in arms, citing among other things, hygiene concerns, especially about the possibility of catching an STD while helping a stranger fill up their car.

Fairytale Town of Twenniga Baynish Discovered in Norway

OSLO, Norway – For generation upon generation, the children of Norway have thrilled to bedtime stories of the fairytale land of Twenniga Baynish, and the population of little magical people that supposedly live there.

According to the legend, Twenniga Baynish is populated by magical gnomes, elves, and genies.

It's a place where the sun is always shining, and everything is always perfect.

There's even one part of the town where all the houses are made of candy and cake, and other assorted sweets.

There's natural fountains of soda that shoot up from the ground, and pools of delicious ice cream, of every flavor imaginable dot the countryside.

No one ever works in Twenniga Baynish. They don't have to. Everyone has everything they want or need. It's utopia.

The people of Twenniga Baynish spend their days just playing and having fun.

Norwegians believe that all children spend time in Twenniga Baynish before they're born, being surrounded by the magic of the people and the town, so that by the time they're born, they're filled with happiness.

"That's why you never see a sad looking baby, . . . even when they're crying," says Olaf Thorssen curator of the Oslo Children's Museum.

Supposedly, all the Twenniga Baynishian's want is to keep their world a private beautiful place, . . . or so it says in the children's stories.

All that privacy may be over now, since Dr. Lars Pedersson, of the Norwegian Institute of Science claims to have actually found Twenniga Baynish in a remote area of Norway, near the Orknejar Forest nearly hidden between two fjords.

Pedersson has been searching for the magical town for over 30 years, because he always felt in his heart that it really existed.

"Twenniga Baynish may seem like it's only for children, but it isn't," he exclaimed. "It appeals to the child in all of us."

Leading a group of scientists on an expedition near Alta Karosjok close to the border of Sweden, Pedersson suddenly became aware of a very strange type of music emanating from the forest.

The way he explained it, "It sounded like a mixture of pipes and flutes. Something you'd hear in a children's movie, only this was real."

He followed the music, but wasn't quite ready for what he encountered. Hundreds, and hundreds of small cartoonish-type beings, dressed in the most colorful clothes, "and what's more, they had magical powers," he said.

"Most, if not all of them could fly," said Pedersson. "You couldn't see their wings when they were standing still, but on a moment's notice, they could suddenly shoot straight up into the air, and fly up into the branches of a tree. They actually hovered like little humming birds. And the laughter was deafening. Constant laughing and chattering."

The people of Twenniga Baynish seemed as interested in him and his group of scientists as the scientists were in them.

Ladislaw Finn, the Chairman of Sociological Studies at NIS, was absolutely overwhelmed with excitement.

"The only thing I could compare it to is going to the North Pole, discovering Santa Claus, and finding out that he's real after all these years."

Asked if he and his men felt safe with these magical creatures, Pedersson responded, "The only danger was to those of my men who were diabetic, being surrounded by all those sweets.

We actually spent the night in a gingerbread house, and in the morning for breakfast, each of the men took a bite out of one of the walls. If I hadn't seen it myself, I never would have believed it."

Man Displays Uncanny Ability To Lift Heavy Objects With His Eye

BUTTE, Montana – Dale Roderick, a hardware store owner in Butte, has just been accepted into the Guiness Book of Records, for being able to lift a table with his eye.

"Why anyone would want to do this is beyond the comprehension of most people," said his wife Irma, but Roderick says "it's been a hobby of his ever since he was a kid." "For some reason," he said, "I always liked to do things with my eye."

He went on to explain, "as a very young child, my parents, . . . like most kid's parents, . . . always told me not to stick foreign objects into my eyes. Until I got older, and understood, I always thought they were referring to things made in other countries.

"So I looked for things made in this country to stick in my eye.

"I started out with regular United States pennies. I had the unusual ability to be able to pick pennies off of a counter top using just my eye.

"I remember, being just about 7 or 8 years old, and my friends would take bets on how many pennies I could lift with my eye. From pennies, I graduated to nickels, then quarters, half dollars, and eventually large silver dollars. My eye carrying capacity was increasing monthly."

Dr. Harold Schvayne, head ophthalmologist at Butte Memorial Hospital, says that what Roderick is doing can be very injurious to one's eyesight, as well as damaging their appearance esthetically. Schvayne explains, "Eyes were meant for seeing, not heavy lifting.

"I myself have often wished I had a third arm, especially when carrying many packages, and fumbling with my door keys, but I would never think of trying to grab one of the packages with my eye. It would be too dangerous."

He went on to say, "Roderick doesn't realize what he's doing, or that he's setting a dangerous example for children."

He added that he's seen other people try this, and the eye that they used for lifting became so muscular, it became distorted, and changed the entire shape of their face, . . . "and not for the better either."

He ended by saying, "even bodybuilders who look to enlarge every possible muscle to it's fullest capacity, never have muscular eyes. There's just no reason for it."

Roderick didn't start lifting furniture with his eye for many years. It took him quite a while until he developed a technique for grasping such large pieces, without using his hands for help.

He claims his eye-lifting talent even helped save his life, and his home once in an emergency. He had broken both of his arms in a gymnastics accident, while trying to show a customer how to do a backflip in the middle of the hardware store.

Subsequently both of his arms wound up in casts. He walked into his house one afternoon, to find that a fire had started in the kitchen, and he had no way to grab his fire extinguisher. Quick as a flash, he managed to grab a water filled bucket with his eye, and put out the fire, saving his home, his ant farm, and all of his belongings.

Buffalo Company Makes Wearable Awnings For People

BUFFALO, New York – Many businesses use awnings routinely both to advertise, and to protect people from getting wet in inclement weather.

Now people can have their own personal awnings to take with them wherever they go, thanks to Pete Gradabowski of Buffalo Shade and Awning.

Pete's brother Joe, the inspiration for this ground-shaking invention, is a hard working door-to-door salesman who was tired of getting sick with colds and viruses from getting soaked during sudden, unexpected rainstorms. Invariably, like many of us, he had forgotten his umbrella, and went to work anyway.

Now that he wears his own personal awning, he hasn't been sick for over a year.

Joe says, "the beauty part is no one can see how it attaches. They're absolutely shocked when the awning unfolds."

The awning sits on top of a pole that is comfortably molded to your back, and slides down under your clothing, or under a suit jacket, anchoring itself with a clip either onto your belt, or onto any undergarment.

The folded up awning rests comfortably on your head until you need it. "It can also be installed inside the peak of a baseball cap, the brim of a fedora, or even a top hat if you're going out formal," says Gradabowski.

A string with a pull chain runs down your arm, and is always accessible to your hand. At the first sign of inclement weather, you pull the chain, and voila, . . . your own personal awning unfolds above your head, protecting you from the elements.

It also comes in a larger model that can accommodate two people standing together under one awning. Perfect for a date.

You can have your awning personalized if you like with the name of your business, or it can say anything you want, just like vanity plates for your car.

Pete, who claims he's known for his sense of humor, wears an awning that says, ""Danger -Shady Character Below," an inventive way to promote his shade business.

His brother Joe, a self-admitted workaholic wears an awning that reads, "No Yawning Under This Awning."

At only $69.99 for the single model, and $89.99 for the double, they're "literally flying off the shelves," says Gradabowski. Pete says his awnings will replace the umbrella, and make it obsolete.

"People lose umbrellas all the time. They're a hassle to hold, especially if your arms are filled with packages. They're just very unwieldy. With an awning, your arms are free to carry packages, you can never lose it, plus they can never blow inside out like a cheap umbrella.

"With an awning, you can walk along in a hurricane, and still stay dry."

Next up for the Gradabowski brothers, ... personal venetian blinds for those intimate cell phone calls, and for anyone else who wants privacy in the street.

Man Removes Own Appendix Using Beer As Anesthetic

BURMINGHAM, Alabama – A man removed his own appendix – but he saved money by doing it himself with handy household items!

Horace Wilfrey, an admitted alcoholic, and proud of it, had been having recurrent pain on his lower right side. Having been a fan of doctor shows his whole life, and having a mother who cleaned hospital rooms, they combined their medical knowledge and came up with a diagnosis.

He knew the liver pain he was used to living with was in the upper right quadrant, so the lower right quadrant could only mean one thing, … appendicitis. His mother concurred.

Realizing the potential danger of acute appendicitis, he decided that surgery would be necessary. Having seen it several times on television, he felt equipped to give it a whirl, and he did, using a full case of beer as an anesthetic.

Downing the entire case in just under an hour, he was already feeling no pain, as they say, and felt sure he was sufficiently anesthetized.

Using an ironing board as an operating table, he compiled his surgical armamentarium, including a can opener, a serrated bread knife, and one of those little forks you use for eating a shrimp cocktail.

Dipping his surgical instruments into his beer to sterilize them, he began the 45 minute procedure.

While his mother held up a make-up mirror, he made his initial incision with the can opener, quickly located his appendix, speared it with the tiny fork, and while his mother held it in place, he used the serrated bread knife to sever it from it's location.

Then using unwaxed dental floss for sutures, he stitched himself up, and spent the rest of the day "just lying back on the couch admiring his handiwork."

Amazingly, he seems to have healed up uneventfully. He feels the alcohol in the beer kept him from getting any infections.

Dr. Erno Hern, noted gastrointestinal surgeon at Belvedere General Hospital in Burmingham said that surgery of this kind is almost unheard of, and that "just because it worked for Wilfrey, people shouldn't get the idea they can just do these kinds of things at home."

"Surgery is not a party game," he went on to say, "it's supposed to be done by trained surgeons, not by drunk men with their mothers."

Wilfrey has offered to teach his technique at the medical school, but so far has received no response.

SHORT BITS

BROTHERS WITH LONGEST POLICE RECORDS IN THE WORLD CLAIM TO BE PROFESSIONAL SCAPEGOATS – What at first appeared to be just a simple candy store robbery turned out not to be so simple when the two brothers accused of the crime unfolded a truly bizarre tale. Hector and Roberto Adalponte, of Arequipa, Peru, have each been arrested thousands of times, and claim to be the only two criminals in their town. That's why they were enraged when someone else's fingerprints supposedly turned up at the crime scene, and the police attempted to arrest another man.

The brothers lodged a formal complaint, explaining that they are professional scapegoats working for the police, and that it is their job to be framed for all crimes whether they committed them or not. They refuse to give anyone else the credit, and demand to be prosecuted for the crime. "We know our rights," said Roberto.

NO MORE WEIGHTS—GYMS FILLED WITH FURNITURE THE NEWEST CRAZE – A hard core group of bodybuilders has actually eschewed the use of weights as being passé. Wayne Conklin, who currently has the biggest arms in the world, verified at 28 inches in circumference, says the new thing in bodybuilding is working out with furniture.

"Anyone can lift weights," he says. "It's much too easy. There's no challenge.

But furniture is a whole other story. Ever see how strong those guys are who move furniture? Try doing three sets of presses with an armoire. That's when you can say you had a real work–out. Just this morning, I worked my back with a Baby Grand piano. In between sets, I practiced my scales. It was amazing." Hey Louie, when you're done with that chest of drawers, pass it over here okay?"

SCREAM YOUR CHILDREN TO SLEEP – Behavioral scientists have just come out with a study that says that putting your child to bed by screaming at them is much better for them than reading them a quiet story or playing quiet, soothing music. They say that screaming them to sleep prepares them for the stressful world they are growing up into, and that they will be much better prepared to handle stress when they've learned to do so as children.

TRAIN YOUR CHILD TO BE RUDE – In a related story childcare experts advise telling your children to do the exact opposite of what you want them to do, because rebellious children tend to do that anyway. So if you want your kids to behave in school give them the exact opposite instructions. From now on instead of telling them to wait their turn, and be polite, tell them instead to push on line, grab food first, never say thank-you, and disrupt the class.

ARABS DEVELOP REAL FLYING CARPETS – Like a page out of the book "Ali Baba," U.S. Intelligence has identified the small, flat unusually shaped UFO's it has been spotting flying above Iraq as flying carpets. It seems the Iraqis have actually developed the technology to make carpets fly, and are using them to attack our soldiers. This technology is literally the most advanced from that region of the world, since the building of the Pyramids.

Most models seem to be solo carpets, while others seem to be two man carpets. There are even rumors of carpets so big, they could accommodate up to 40 men, and could be considered "wall to wall."

The U.S. is trying to figure out the technology, and where they are able to hide their weapons, while still maneuvering the carpet at speeds of up to 18 miles per hour.

The pilots seem well trained, and are able to swoop down, flying well below our radar, to inflict their damage. When out of regular ammunition, they have been known to throw old fruit and babaganoush.

HOLDING YOUR OWN HAND TO AVOID LONELINESS – Psychologists say that loneliness is the greatest killer of people by far, leading to stress-related illness, and depression, and may even be the cause of certain types of cancer. Physical touch can often be the catalyst to alleviate the loneliness, but some people are so alone, they don't even know any one to touch. That's why doctors are suggesting holding your own hand to feel connected again. More people do this than were formerly believed, as evidenced by the scores of men you see walking with their hands clasped behind their backs. It's a much less obvious way to hold your own hand.

The technique always requires asking yourself permission first before grabbing your own hand. This raises self-esteem, and lends an air of self-respect to the deed, so that you don't just take it for granted that you would hold your own hand.

REAL LIVE SUPERMAN FOILS BANK ROBBERY IN KANSAS – A 30-something man on line at the bank, used what appeared to be super powers to foil a bank robbery in Kansas yesterday.

The gang had ordered all the customers to lie flat on the ground, and was attempting to lock the bank employees in the vault, when one of the gang got nervous and started shooting.

This seemingly mild-mannered man surprised the gang, by suddenly turning into a "Superman," blocking their bullets with his hands, and bending their guns into pretzels.

Whirling around at eye-blurring speed, he then tied them all up with some spare phone cable that was lying around, leaving the robbers for the police to arrest, and leaving everyone else with their mouths gaping open in shock.

Then, before anyone knew what was happening, he ran outside, and leaped up into the air, flying off into the sky.

Police, and customers of the bank seem baffled to explain. One of the tellers exclaimed, "It happened so fast, he never even made his deposit."

WORLD'S MOST DANGEROUS DWARF – Harold Blount may look like a pushover at 4'3" tall, but don't try and take advantage of him if you know what's good for you.

He's a 6th degree Black belt, and takes great pleasure in beating huge guys to a pulp. He's become the most sought after bodyguard in Hollywood, protecting big stars like Sylvester Stallone, Bruce Willis, and even Arnold Schwartzenegger, who claims that if he ever holds office again, he will bring Blount with him.

Blount comes from a long line of dangerous dwarves.

His father, Earl Blount, known as Earl "The Count" Blount, for the long black cape he always wore, was also known for his flying kicks. He was said to be able to kick so high, he once flipped over his own head, and still knocked out his opponent.

His uncle Ike "The Pincer" Blount was able to use his legs like a pair of pliers, and would grip onto his opponent's abdomen, pinching them tightly until they gave up.

DEAN OF WELL KNOWN MEDICAL SCHOOL MUGS STUDENT AT KNIFEPOINT – Students and faculty alike were shocked at Rochester Medical College when it was determined that Dean Orville Lantz was picked out of a line-up, and positively identified as the man who mugged foreign exchange student Abner Habubbi during a school celebration last week-end.

Lantz allegedly got away with only about 14 or 15 dollars, but he threatened to come after Habubbi, and his family if he said anything about the incident.

It seems the trouble all started when Habubbi was coming down the stairs on a break during the festivities, and the Dean stopped him and asked him for a quarter.

Habubbi refused, and as he turned to leave, the Dean kicked him, as he put it, . . . "right in the rear end."

Habubbi protested, and the next thing he knew, the Dean pulled a switchblade knife on him, put it to his throat, and took all of his money.

The Dean claims it was all a mistake. He said he was just showing the student how to hold a scalpel during thyroid surgery, when the student took out his wallet, and literally "forced me to take whatever money was inside."

He assumed he was giving him the money out of gratitude for what he had just been teaching him.

Authorities say the Dean has never been in trouble before, and are weighing probation rather than jail time if, and when he's found guilty.

CONGRESSMEN CAUGHT TOWEL DANCING – Two as yet unnamed Congressmen, one Republican, one Democrat, were caught after hours in the shower room of the Congressional gym, dancing naked to loud hip-hop music and whipping each other with wet towels.

Lawyers for the Congressmen claim they were working overtime, preparing for a trip to an also as yet unnamed nation where this type of behavior is not only tolerated, but expected.

Towel Dancing became popular on college campuses throughout the country, during the mid-to late 80s, but died out by the early 90s.

It surfaced again on Wall Street during the tech boom of the late 90s, however this is the first time it has been reported to have occurred within institutions of government.

The President has steadfastly refused to make any comments on these accusations of Towel Dancing until all the facts are in.

MAN ROBS BANK USING A Q-TIP AS A WEAPON – Security guards at banks are usually very aware of all types of weapons. John Dillinger used a gun, as did Bonnie and Clyde. Some criminals have used knives, an axe, or even an ice pick. Strange as it sounds, one even used his chin. Criminals have always thought of ingenious ways of separating banks from their money, but in the annals of crime, no one has ever used a Q-Tip. Until Thelonius Bragg came along and changed the game. Thelonius Bragg jammed a Q-Tip into the ear of a bank manager, and threatened to "push really hard" unless he opened up the safe, and gave him what he wanted. The bank manager remembering what his mother taught him as a child, to never push a Q-Tip too far into his ear, complied with Bragg's wishes. Bragg got away with over fifty thousand dollars. The Bank manager lost some hearing in the assault.

NIGHT LIFE IMPRESARIO INJURED MAKING ENTRANCE BY SLINGSHOT – The New York nightlife scene is a very competitive one to break into. Club-owners, hungry for a piece of the huge entertainment pie, try and outdo each other in an attempt to make a name for themselves. One unfortunate impresario went a little too far, and almost lost his life in the process.

Famed club-owner Howard Sanz wanted to really make an entrance at the opening of his new Manhattan dance club, called "Itch." He planned to make his arrival by being launched into a throne-like chair by a specially made slingshot, used only by highly trained circus performers. Unfortunately the calculations went awry, and he flew over the chair by a foot, crashing through his brand new plate glass window, sustaining serious injuries and almost ending his illustrious career.

He literally got more than scratched at "Itch."

MAN ACCIDENTALLY KILLS HIMSELF PLAYING CAT'S CRADLE – Whoever thought a simple child's game could be so dangerous? Certainly not Elmont Wiggins when he agreed to an all out game of "Cat's Cradle." In the world's first tragedy involving the child's game of string passing, known as "Cat's Cradle," Elmont Wiggins accidentally hung himself trying to get out of a highly difficult move. His partner had managed to pass Wiggins the string with both hands, known as the "Fish In The Box," but as Wiggins struggled to untangle himself, he had just about succeeded, when the string accidentally looped around his neck, and as he twisted his hands, he slowly choked himself to death.

MAN LOSES LEGS TO TIGHT PANTS – Baby boomers who wore tight pants back in the day, are now starting to show the effects of the lack of circulation caused by the skintight styles of the '60s and '70s. Steve Hrabofsky had been wearing tight pants since 1963 despite style changes to the contrary, and he finally paid the price.

Despite pleas from well meaning friends who tried to get him to switch to baggies, Steve insisted on staying with skintight pants, and the lack of circulation over all those years, finally caused gangrene, and led to the loss of his legs from the dreaded condition known as PRG, . . . "Pants-Related Gangrene."

COMING ON TIME – (ORGASMS CURE THE CHRONICALLY LATE) – A Belgian surgeon, Dr. Matthias Blechner, has come up with a new plan to cure chronic lateness, utilizing an outdated form of technology, the lowly pager. He feels he can cure lateness, by associating being on time with something pleasurable, namely an orgasm.

He developed a combination pager/vibrator that gets surgically implanted near the groin. You give the person expecting you your pager number, and about an hour before you're due to arrive, they page you over and over again, until you reach a state of satisfaction. The pleasure principal drives you to be on time."

NEW FASHION WRINKLE – UNDERHATS; SEXY UNDERWEAR FOR YOUR HEAD – Hot models often like to wear hats, but after a night of sweaty dancing, how do you avoid dreaded "hat hair?" According to designer Dallas Montgomery, the new anti-hat-hair accessory is underhats, . . . sexy underwear for your head. Sexy, silky, see through, they even come in a thong, where the string runs down the center of your face. One model said, "I thought panty-hose were fragile, but every time I run my fingers through my hair, I get a run in my underhat."

CONFUSED FARMER PLANTS COTTON AND LITTLE STICKS, IN ATTEMPT TO GROW Q-TIPS – Harold Loomis of Macon, Georgia has a thousand acre farm where he grows many things including cotton, but after two weeks on a new anti-depressant he began to get strange thoughts, says his wife Irma. "He said he began to see the world in a new way," said his wife of 40 years. She quoted Loomis as saying that "farmers had a particular gift to give to the world, a knack for growing things, and he felt it was his purpose to do something special along those lines. He wanted to do something to "give back," as he put it. Then he said something about Q-Tips, and he got all excited."

What Loomis said was that "people in the United States have so many things they take for granted, but people in third world countries don't have even the simplest things, like Q-Tips." He decided to do something about it.

"The next thing I knew he began to plant cotton, and small pieces of wood in the same hole determined to grow Q-Tips and donate them to third world countries. I don't know how to break it to him. I guess we'll have to wait until the Spring."

THROWING THE BOOK AT HIM – (NEW YORK POLICE TO BE EQUIPPED WITH OBJECTS TO THROW AT PEOPLE) – In an effort to cut down on reports of police brutality in inner city neighborhoods, the police themselves have come up with what they think is a brilliant idea. Instead of shooting guns at people, they will be allowed to throw various items at suspected felons, to keep them from getting away. On the list of proposed items is a baseball, an ash tray, the proverbial book, an empty bottle of wine, darts, and an item expected to be favored by many female police, especially those who are fans of old comedy films . . . a frying pan. One officer even suggested training cops to actually throw bullets at people, but he added, "You'd have to throw them really hard in order for them to have any effect!"

DENTIST USES SHARK BIOLOGY TO GIVE PEOPLE TEETH THAT GROW BACK – Dr. Reginald Whitmyer, an oral/maxillo-facial surgeon from White Plains, New York claims to have succeeded in isolating the shark gene that makes multiple sets of teeth grow, and has implanted that gene into the mouths of edentulous patients. Within several months, each of the transplant recipients started teething, and grew a new set of teeth. One man's wife said that since her husband had the procedure done he's been very happy, but his eating habits have changed completely. She explained, "he no longer uses utensils. He snatches his steak off the plate with just his jaws and teeth, and then shakes his head back and forth until he rips a piece off. It's been very disconcerting in front of the children," she says.

HELP ME, I'M MELTING – For over two hundred years, Madame Tussaud's wax museum has been one of the top five tourist attractions in London. More than 2.7 million people pass through it's doors each year, however one of those 2.7 million people seems to have a very strange sense of humor. Last week, workers at the world famous museum were horrified to find that someone had snuck in overnight while the museum was closed, and attached a wick to each one of the 1018 statues currently on display. Henry Finsterbeck, spokesman/caretaker for the museum said that just the sight of all those wicks was a nightmare for all concerned. "One lunatic with a cigarette lighter, and it would have been all over. Like one giant birthday cake with the candles disguised as human beings."

MAN WRITES LONGEST LOVE LETTER IN HISTORY – A man in Sydney, Australia wrote his girlfriend in Spain, the longest love letter in history. Albert Forrager wrote a 4000 page letter to his fiance Emily Hern to tell her how much he loved her. It was to be read before they got married. She received the letter when she was 38. Half way through reading it, she died of old age.

CHIROPRACTORS ADVISE WEARING SWIM FINS FOR BACK PAIN – Something about the stability of wearing swim fins seems to relieve the painful, debilitating symptoms of sciatica. Chiropractors all over the country have been advising their sciatic patients to wear swim fins to the office, especially if their job involves a lot of standing. One cardiac surgeon was reported to be wearing swim fins in the operating room, and several undercover policemen have been seen wearing them while assigned to long, arduous stake-outs. According to one of the detectives, an additional benefit of wearing fins, is added traction when chasing perpetrators through the snow.

ALLIGATOR SUITS TO GO WITH ALLIGATOR SHOES – Men who pride themselves on dressing well usually have at least one pair of alligator shoes, with matching accessories like an alligator wallet, and/or an alligator belt. Now they can have the whole thing. A designer in Rome, Norberto Catalucci, has come up with an entire suit made out of alligator skin. The three piece suit, complete with alligator vest, also comes with a complimentary pair of alligator socks. The price may be prohibitive, as well as illegal in some places where alligators are considered a protected species.

SALMON UPSETTING ECOSYSTEM BY TEACHING OTHER FISH TO SWIM UPSTREAM – Salmon, known to be fairly docile, non-aggressive type fish, are probably best known for their uncanny ability to swim upstream to spawn. Lately, they have been upsetting the ecosystem of the country's rivers by subversively teaching other types of fish to swim upstream to spawn as well. Trout, walleye, carp, and northern pike, have been seen struggling to make their way upstream, but because it's so new to them, they often get lost, and become injured. Several fish have actually been reported to have drowned. Marine biologist, Dr. Harry Veuvre feels that these subversive salmon are just a genetic abnormality, and do not pose a long-term threat to our nation's fish supply. In other words, . . . no pun intended, these salmon are just a fluke!

TAILOR WHO TAPERS PEOPLE – A tailor and a plastic surgeon have joined forces to create what they refer to as custom made people. Dr. Joao Ristangao of Brazil, and Marco D'Arranzio, a tailor from Philadelphia met while D'Arranzio was vacationing in Brazil. Ristingao complimented D'Arranzio on the cut of his suit, and when D'Arranzio admitted to having made it himself, Ristingao said that a lightbulb went off in his head, and their company called Snippit was born.

Patients are put under general anesthesia, and then D'Arranzio places chalk marks and pins where he wants Ristangao to cut. Ristangao explains, "A good tailor has an amazing eye for detail, sometimes even better than a plastic surgeon. He's used to altering clothing to make people look their best. The only difference in our work is that pants don't bleed. So he makes the marks, and I do the alterations. I couldn't ask for a better partner."

WOMEN WHO MASSAGE FRUIT – China must by necessity import most of it's apples, strawberries, and grapes, as much of it's land does not support the growth of fruit. However, it seems to have an abundance of a certain type of pear, especially in the city of Chun Lao in southern China. This small city is known for the magical quality of it's Shandong Pear, which legend attributes to the fact that the women of that city have for centuries, engaged in the ancient ritual art of fruit massage.

Centuries ago, when fruit was very scarce in China, it was believed that the fruit wouldn't grow because it was nervous, and the best way to calm it down, would be the same way you would calm down a nervous person, through the use of massage.

Women would go to the pear trees, and gently massage the pears while they were still attached. When it was time to gather the pears from the trees, the women would massage them again, thereby supposedly transferring powerful energy to the pears, that in turn would be transferred to whoever ate the pear. The sale of those pears was the major source of income for the people of Chun Lao, and sustained them through some very rough times. That is why fruit massage is carried on to this day.

WOMAN WHO KNITS FURNITURE – Hattie May Swayne, of Roseville, Arkansas claims to be the first woman in the world with an entire household of hand-knit furniture. She claims she started knitting furniture as a child, because "everyone knit sweaters, or scarves, and that was just so boring." She began with a simple ottoman for her mother to use to rest her feet on after a long day working on the family farm. As she got older, and was able to afford more yarn, she began knitting larger pieces, like a chair, then a table, and finally worked her way up to an armoire, and a king-size bed. The furniture is reinforced with Popsicle sticks, held together with rubber bands for support, and according to Hattie May can support the weight of a 250 pound man.

HYSTERICAL BALDNESS IS SWEEPING THE COUNTRY – You've heard of hysterical blindness, and hysterical deafness. Now there's "hysterical baldness." Men across the country have been going to bed with a full head of hair, and waking up as smooth as a cue ball. Thought to be caused by intense stress, most of the men involved are stock traders.

Arlo Vank, CEO of Rockport Securities in Metairie, Louisiana claims he had a thick head of hair "like a wild man," and after a particularly stressful day of trading, he woke up the next morning, glanced to his right, and thought a cat had climbed into bed with him, and went to sleep on his pillow."

"I reached over to pet it," he continued, "and it turned out to be my hair. I was so bald, you could have stuck your fingers in my nose and mouth and used my head as a bowling ball."

The men are being advised to quit their jobs in hopes that their hair might come back even before the economy does.

BEACHCOMBER PUTS SEASHELL TO HIS EAR, AND GETS SECRET WHITE HOUSE CALLS – Mack Binney, an itinerant beachcomber from Hawaii, survives by selling tourists interesting shells he finds on the beach.

He got the shock of his life recently, as he found an unusually patterned shell, put it to his ear, and instead of hearing the roar of the ocean, found himself tapping into high security calls from the White House. Recognizing the voice on the shell to be that of Pres. Obama, he immediately called a local FBI office, to report the incident. The first five times, the FBI hung up, thinking it was a practical joker, or just some nut. After the fifth call, they sent agents out to cart Binney off to a loony bin. Before they hauled him away, he was able to convince them to listen to the shell, where they were also shocked to hear Pres. Obama's private calls to foreign dignitaries. Scientists are now examining the shell to try and explain how something like this could happen.

WOMAN IMPREGNATED THROUGH ORAL SEX – Hermina Walnute made medical history by being the first woman ever to become pregnant through oral sex. The woman insists that she never had regular sex because she was always told that oral sex was the safest. Interestingly enough, the swelling of the pregnancy started in her throat and neck, and she thought at first that she was developing a goiter. As the swelling moved slowly downward, and developed a heartbeat, her gynecologist, Dr. Randall Whitely confirmed that indeed she was pregnant. He said he had never seen anything like this before, and couldn't really explain how it happened. Whitely added, "If the pregnancy had stayed up high where it was, she would have literally felt like that old expression, "her heart was in her mouth."

THE VIKINGS WERE CHINESE – Usually portrayed as being tall and blonde, there's new evidence to the contrary that the Vikings were actually Chinese. They may not have started out that way, but by the 12th century, that's how things wound up. Beginning as early as the 9th century, there are reports linking the Vikings with Asia, for trading purposes. As opposites tend to attract, there were large numbers of marriages between the Scandinavian warriors, and the Asian people they dealt with. As a result, so many Viking babies were born with Asian features, that by the time of the 12th century, most of the Vikings were Chinese and had to wear blonde wigs to keep up the image. By the 13th century, it's reported that all of the Vikings were at that point actually Chinese.

HUGE TURTLES USED AS GUARD DOGS – When most people think of a turtle, they think of the little ones with the painted shells that you get for a couple of dollars at a carnival or a pet shop, and that move very slowly. Well think again. Now there's a turtle whose size averages four feet across, and can run at about 14 miles per hour, making them even faster than a squirrel. They were discovered living in the oceans off the Azores, which some anthropologists and archaeologists feel may be part of the lost continent of Atlantis. The turtles seem to be intelligent, are able to be domesticated, and are very protective of their young, to the point that the islanders use them as pets and for protection. They have a beak and jaws almost as powerful as a pit bull. Because of that, wealthy people in the United States have begun using them instead of guard dogs, because they eat a lot less, and make a lot less noise.

BASKETBALL PLAYER FROM CHINA HAS ABILITY TO BOUNCE – Sports reporters often talk about players with "rubber legs," but a basketball player from China who literally has the ability to bounce has caught the attention of sports agents from all over the world. Reportedly due to rubberized implants that were placed in his legs to give him flexibility after a childhood accident, Hong Chi Wong, at 6'9" tall, has legs so flexible that they seem to bend both ways at the same time. His ability to leap vertically measures over 56", in a game where 40" is considered amazing. When he takes a jump shot there's no one on any team who could block him. Other players may scream "foul," but there seems to be nothing illegal about it because he's using his own legs. Wong is from the Fujian Province, in China, where Fu means "lucky" and "Jian" means "duck" and whichever team gets him will be exactly that !

CELL PHONE CONNECTION TO OUTER SPACE – It seems that alien beings are trying to contact us through our cell phones. Certain brands of phones have reported picking up text messages from what appear to be UFO's in outer space. Star 69 does not seem to work as far as returning the calls goes, because our cell phones are not intergalactic. As a matter of fact, most people are glad when they work in their own neighborhoods. With most of the cell phone companies vying for the public's business, they're not sure whether to advertise this as a special feature of a new offering plan, like 400 anytime minutes, free nights and weekends, and unlimited earth to UFO messages, or whether it might just be better not to say anything about it at all.

Airforce Colonel H.P. Briggs went on record as saying that there is no official proof that these are extra-terrestrials who are trying to contact us, and feels it may be the work of "pranksters, with a highly advanced knowledge of digital technology."

INNOCENT MAN RE-HEADED AFTER GUILLOTINING – The French influenced country of Morocco is one of the last places in the world that still uses the guillotine to execute it's criminals. In the United States, many people are opposed to capital punishment because there is no recourse if the accused is eventually proved to be innocent. Once you've lost your head, it's assumed it's too late, unless you're Ahmoud Abboud.

Abboud was beheaded in a marketplace in Morocco, just as they did three hundred years ago, but within seconds of the beheading, just as his head rolled into the basket, someone came forward with evidence that would have cleared his name.

As luck would have it, a neurosurgeon happened to be present, wrapped the head in ice, applied a tourniquet to the neck, and raced the body to a nearby hospital to try and re-attach the head.

After 16 hours of surgery, the head was re-attached, and aside from "feeling a little dizzy every once in a while," Abboud has regained most of his functions. He says he hides the scar by wearing a tie. In Morocco, that must stand out more than a 360 degree scar on your neck.

FACIAL HAIR FOR DOGS – Dogs are only allowed to stay in a pound for a certain amount of time. If they are not adopted within that time, they are often put to sleep. Dog lovers are always wondering what they can do to make certain dogs more likely to be adopted, and a dog shelter in Maine believes it has the answer : Doggy Beards. Veterinarian, Dr. Alan Shwampsky explains, "We can't really explain why, but the bearded breeds like the Schnauzers, the Sheep Dogs, and the Pomeranians seem to be adopted much quicker than say the beardless dogs like the Labradors, the Pinschers, or the German Shepherds. I noticed that trend over many years and decided to make a little test. I created a small beard for a Doberman Pinscher that was about to be put down, and within 2 days he had a home. Ever since that time, I make small beards for all of my beardless dogs, and the results are astounding. Every single dog gets adopted." Schwampsky added, "Some of the dogs resist the beard at first, because the elastic band annoys them, but they wind up getting used to it."

SPEAKING POLISH – Few people know that one of the reasons Poland is called Poland, is because in ancient days, people spoke to each other through short poles. They were called "speaking poles" and almost resembled the cardboard tubes from the center of a roll of paper towels. The custom was instituted by a king named Wenceslas III in the year 1178. Towns in Poland in those days were extremely noisy, and the king felt that people were having a hard time hearing each other over all the tumult. Therefore he ruled that if all people spoke through small poles it would direct, and channel the voice, and make it easier to hear. People had pole holders that attached to their belts, and when they wanted to speak to someone they pulled out their pole, and spoke into it. For the most part, speaking poles went out of use in the late 18th century, but every once in awhile, even today, they tend to crop up among the elderly residents of the smaller towns.

QUILL PENS MAKING A COMEBACK – Not since the days of John Hancock have quill pens been used with such regularity as on the campus of USC, in southern California. Known for being the home of many past unusual trends such as leather socks with heels and laces, wooden gloves, and books made of glass, students are turning up all over signing phony documents for each other written on parchment, and signed with a quill pen. Quill pens are usually made from an ostrich feather, and then dipped in an inkwell before writing with the hard tip of the feather. One unfortunate student , who didn't know that quill pens were made from feathers, was almost killed trying to make a quill pen using the quills of a live uncooperative porcupine.

MAN ATTEMPTS TO SHAKE HANDS WITH EVERY PERSON IN INDIA – As of the 2001 census, the population of India stood at over 1 billion, 27 million people. Harold Flyman of Minnesota, took that as a challenge. Believing in the importance of touch as a way of uniting people, he decided to try and shake hands with every single person in India, and for the last 15 years, seven days a week, from the hours of 7 A.M. until 11 P.M. that's exactly what he has done.

Scientists and mathematicians have calculated that as long as the country can keep their birthrate under control, Flyman could accomplish his task in another two to three more years. The other variable factor is how the skin on Flyman's hands is holding up.

Politicians can attest to the fact that constant handshaking takes a tremendous toll on the skin of the hands.

The trauma varies according to the type of handshake. Over the last 15 years, Flyman has seen considerable changes in what is considered acceptable as a handshake.

In the late 80s and early 90s, "slapping someone five," wasn't all that bad," he says, but in the larger Indian cities that have been influenced more by America, the newly created "fist bump" has become considerably painful. In Flyman's own words, "things were going fine until I hit a town of 80,000 that was into the hip-hop inspired fist bump. My hand will never be the same".

EMERGENCY LIBRARIANS CUT DOWN ON VIOLENCE – Most people don't consider being a librarian to be dangerous, or physically demanding work. Say hello to the men and women of the ELC, the Elite Library Corps, a group of specially trained librarians being used in the nation's new attempt to serve the emergency library needs of the public, thereby cutting down on book related violence.

Evelyn Tarnofsky, head of the ELC, explains that many people, frustrated with confusing card catalogues, and microfiche machines, have shied away from libraries for many years, and are often led to crimes of violence due to their frustration.

Then there are the people who find it hard to sleep at night, and who suddenly find themselves craving a particular book, hoping it will put them to sleep. Finding most bookstores, and all libraries closed, they realize they have nowhere to turn, and too often they become violent.

This corps of emergency librarians is dedicated to cutting down on book-related violence, by making books available to the public on a 24 hour a day basis. They are all highly trained in martial arts, especially in close hand-to-hand combat.

Each large city will soon have one library that will stay open all night, manned by these elite, highly trained, and very brave librarians.

FACE READING – Classes in what is known as "face reading" have been popping up all over the country, where people experienced in Healing and energy work try and enlighten you about yourself by feeling parts of your face, and examining your physiognomy. Learning to do face reading is a tedious, and difficult task. Problems have arisen around exam time, when one student may be heard asking another, "May I please borrow your face. I have a test in the morning, and I need to study!"

Other problems involve reading a face that you've already read, but not realizing it until you are half way through. "I knew it felt familiar, I just couldn't place where I've read it before."

ALLERGIC ARCHAEOLOGIST ACCIDENTALLY BLOWS HIS NOSE IN PRICELESS TISSUE – A rare, ancient tissue, thought to be from around the era of Jesus Christ has been thoughtlessly ruined when an archeologist with a bad cold, accidentally blew his nose in it. Herve Grandeur had caught a cold from being out on the desert digging up artifacts, when one of his men ran over excitedly waving what Grandeur took to be just an ordinary tissue. He had no idea his colleague had just unearthed it from a dig. Just at that moment, Grandeur felt the need to sneeze, and before his astonished colleague could scream, "Sacre Bleu," the priceless tissue was ruined.

Only once before has something like this happened, when a drunken archaeologist accidentally urinated in a pair of pants from the Stone Age. They may have been the very first pair of pants in the world.

He claims he had just put the pants on to try and keep warm, when he fell asleep due to the effects of the alcohol, and accidentally ruined the pants.

SITTING BULL HAD TO STAND – Lakota Medicine Man and Tribal Chief, Sitting Bull, was recognized in American history as being the last Sioux Indian to surrender to the U.S. Government in 1881. He was given the Indian name Tatanka-Iyotanka, which translates as a buffalo bull sitting intractably on its haunches. The only problem is it has come to light that Sitting Bull never actually sat.

He suffered with severe back problems that caused him to have to stay in a half sitting, half reclining position, and most of the time he actually stood.

The problem was that there was no Indian translation for the words "Standing Bull," or even "Leaning To One Side Bull," so he went down in history as Sitting Bull.

When sleeping, he had his wife strap him to a pole in his teepee, and spent most nights sleeping erect on his feet, standing up. Historians now realize it would have been more accurate to refer to him as "Semi-Reclining Bull."

OVERZEALOUS LOVERS CAN DAMAGE PARTNER'S NERVOUS SYSTEM – Blowing in someone's ear used to be thought of as romantic in some circles, but doctors are now saying that if done in excess, it can cause something known as a "brain cold," or a "brain freeze," that can turn out to be fatal.

At the very least, it can disturb the balance of the inner ear, causing the recipient of the attention to experience vertigo, and lose their equilibrium.

Many overzealous lovers have been taking credit for effects like that, telling the object of their affections that they are just "in a swoon," and feel dizzy from the power of the attention, but the truth is that intense blowing into the ear is not good for the stapes, one of the tiny bones that is needed for hearing, and for equilibrium. These same doctors advise these overzealous lovers to try using a small plastic funnel or tube, to direct the blown air into a safer part of the ear, and not directly down into the ear canal.

GOVERNMENT USING INVISIBLE MEN – The government has developed a little blue pill that allows it's operatives to become invisible. Sources have told us that several of our invisible men have already been sent behind enemy lines in Iraq, with some sources claiming we have an entire division of invisible soldiers. Some believe that Joe Biden has been the guinea pig for the research, which might explain why he's often so hard to find. They hope to be able to keep the drug out of the hands of current, and aspiring politicians who seem to have a hard time keeping their hands to themselves even when they're visible. If they were invisible, many fear that no woman would be safe.

RESTAURANT THAT SERVES FUMES – In an effort to counteract the fact that people on diets tend to overeat in restaurants, a group of doctors came up with something totally new in weight loss, a restaurant that only serves the scent of food, but not the food itself.

You can order anything you're in the mood for, and through the miracle of technology, instead of bringing you the food, the waiter brings you stained plates and used silverware, scented with the food of your choice, to make you feel like you already ate. They even supply used napkins. The only thing real is the bill. You pay for what you ordered, even though you didn't get to eat it. If you don't lose weight in this restaurant, you probably never will.

MAN DYES FISH TO MATCH HIS SUIT – A man with an unusual sense of style showed up at a trendy nightclub in London carrying a fish sticking out of his handkerchief pocket instead of a silk handkerchief. The fish was dyed blue to match his suit. By the end of the week, the craze had caught on, and nightclubbers all over London were dyeing fish to match their suits.

Animal rights activists have declared war on the fish wearers, insisting that fish were not meant to be worn, but fish wearers say they are using already dead fish, and should be allowed to wear whatever they want. In terms of chivalry, no one explained what you would do if a woman was in tears and needed your handkerchief. Would you hand her a fish? The bizarre trend just turned up at a club in L.A.

DEODORANT MADE FROM MANURE – Ambergris, the waxy, grayish substance found floating in tropical seas, has long been an ingredient in most perfumes. Truth be told, the substance is actually a secretion from the intestines of sperm whales, which is regurgitated into the ocean, making it in effect, a sort of "whale vomit". Now the manufacturers of deodorants have caught on, and a major cosmetics company in France has discovered a way to use horse manure to make deodorant. They're using a substance found in the manure to make scented deodorant. Coincidentally, France is the home of the only ambergris processing plant in the world. The French seem to be the world's experts in manure and vomit.

Historian Vladimir Von Verne says, "It goes back to the days of the French Revolution when soldiers in the field who could not bathe, discovered that rubbing bird manure into their hair acted as a cleansing/conditioning agent, and rubbing horse manure into their skin acted as an exfoliant." He went on to add, "Ever since that time, the French have been full of s _ _ t!"

So the next time that someone tells you that you smell like s _ _ _, it may turn out to be a compliment! Other planned products are toothpaste made from rat manure, mouthwash made from cat urine, and skin cream from orangutan phlegm.

INFANT MARTIAL ARTIST – A six month old infant in Westchester County seems to be channeling the spirit of an ancient Japanese martial artist, who lived in 7th century Japan. When upset, the infant kicks so hard he breaks his wooden crib. He's already injured both of his parents, and loosened his grandfather's two front teeth with a head butt.

Police have been called to the scene every week since the infant arrived from Japan four months ago. It often takes three grown men to restrain him, and two cops have been injured in the process. Even before he was born, he kicked so hard in the womb that his mother had to be hospitalized. His parents are afraid to let him get hungry, because when he's in a bad mood, anything could happen.

REAL ESTATE AGENT ARRESTED FOR SELLING SMALL, UNUSUALLY SHAPED APARTMENTS – Reasonably priced New York apartments are hard to come by, but this is ridiculous. New York real estate broker Todd Thurn was arrested for taking one two bedroom apartment, and breaking it up into six small geometric shapes, trying to pass them off and sell them as separate "avant-garde" apartments.

Thurn duped buyers, most of whom were from out of town, into believing that this was the new "hip" thing in New York, unusually shaped apartments with no amenities. Some were triangular, and one was like a trapezoid, with no windows, or electrical outlets. Tenants were forced to crouch in the dark.

Some tenants realized before it was too late, but for Herb and Myra Fintz, originally from Tennessee, it wasn't until after their closing that they realized that they had been taken. Thurn as expected, pled "Not Guilty." Mrs. Fintz is suing for a bad back caused by having to crouch in the dark for the two months it took them to figure out that not all New Yorkers live that way.

MAN KILLED IN IRONING ACCIDENT – Harold Mumford, 49, on his way to a dressy social event, had just gotten soaked after being caught in a sudden, unexpected rainstorm. He ran home to change, only to realize he was wearing his only suit.

Already 45 minutes late, he thought he might save time by trying to iron it while it was still on. Lying down on the floor seemed the best approach, but in the midst of ironing the lapels, he got an unexpected phone call from an old girlfriend, and stayed on too long. He left the iron sitting on his chest, and by the time he realized his mistake, the iron had burned it's way into his heart. It was the town's first death due to an ironing accident in many years.

ELDERLY MAN TOURS EUROPE ON POGO-STICK – Armand Karoujian, 87, an elegant man who always wears a tuxedo, has managed to hop through Western Europe on a pogo-stick, carrying nothing more than a knapsack on his back. In the designer knapsack, he managed to squeeze a spare pair of undershorts, a toothbrush, and an extra tuxedo. He says that not enough athletes dress well while engaging in their sport, which he interprets as "a clear lack of respect for their sport and their fans."

He goes on to say, "even if it's not black tie, there's absolutely no reason why all athletes, even tennis players, can not at least wear a coat and tie while engaging in their respective sports. That's why they call it a "sport jacket" because it was meant to wear while playing sports.

For himself, he feels that wearing formal attire while he hops lends an air of respect to a sport that means so much to him. Karoujian's doctor, Dr. Millard Schworman, says that all the pogo stick hopping has done him good. "The last time I examined him," Schworman said, "he had the ureters and kidneys of a 30 year old man."

RETIRED LOCKSMITH COVERS HIMSELF IN POSTAGE STAMPS FOR WORLD UNITY – In what appears to be a misguided effort to promote world unity, Oswald Ningler, a retired locksmith, leaves his house every day without a stitch of clothing on, his body covered only by postage stamps from every country in the world. Ningler says, "the stamps are a symbol of unity. The way they stick together is the way people of all countries should stick together. Let them learn from the stamps."

Herb Pfinster, world famous philatelist says that Ningler is way off base. "What he's doing to these stamps is a travesty. He happens to have a very rare stamp in the center of his back, and probably has no idea what he's doing to the value of it every time he sits down."

PILOT ATTEMPTS TRANS-ATLANTIC FLIGHT USING ONLY HIS BEARD TO CONTROL THE PLANE – Jacques Picard, internationally known daredevil, pilot, and explorer, is known as much for his almost three foot long beard, as he is for his affinity for danger. He has come up with a plan to get into the Guinness Book of Records for being the first man ever to cross the Atlantic flying only with his beard.

He has driven high speed Formula 1 racing cars with his beard, but he's never flown before using that method.

He's quite proud of his two foot eight inch beard, which he keeps waxed into a tapered point. He often uses it while lecturing, either as a pointer, or to get the class's attention, by tapping it on a desk or lectern.

He once attempted to balance on the point of his beard while walking a tightrope attached to the Eiffel Tower, and another time, actually used it as a cane, when he sprained his ankle in a diving accident.

He plans to wrap his beard around the steering column of his plane, using only the movements of his head and neck to control the flight of the plane.

He works out for hours every day doing only neck exercises, which accounts for his 28 inch neck, and says he's not really worried once he gets in the air, it's the take-off and landing that he's most concerned about.

CONTACTED FROM AFTERLIFE BY GREAT GRANDFATHER'S MOUSTACHE – Oleg Schwilling casually opened his wallet to pay for a meal when he was shocked to find a handlebar moustache mixed in with his important papers. Trying his best to maintain his composure, he paid his bill and left.

After leaving the restaurant filled with curiosity, he hurried back to his office to try it on, and found the moustache to be a perfect fit. Like it was custom made for him.

He somehow felt the need to tell his mother, who produced a photograph of Schwilling's great grandfather wearing the exact same type of moustache. Schwilling feels it's a sign that his great grandfather is trying to contact him.

In the meantime, he keeps the moustache safely in his wallet, and only wears it on important occasions while awaiting word from the great beyond.

DENTISTS UNITE AGAINST THE DENTAL HAT – Dentists across the nation are in an uproar over pending legislation that would force them to wear a hat while they were providing their services.

The government says that too many people are afraid of going to the dentist. The same way that people trust policemen, and firemen who are known for wearing hats, the government thinks that if dentists wore hats, more people would feel comfortable, and take advantage of their services. The style and shape of the hat have yet to be determined.

Dentists are threatening to sue, saying it would make them look ridiculous, and that they would be the laughing stock of the medical profession.

One angry dentist queries, "Would they be brightly colored hats with a big "D" on them? How about a chin strap to hold them in place? I'd rather give up my license than have to wear a stupid hat all day in the office. It's ridiculous, and I just won't do it."

WORLD'S LARGEST FOREIGN SOCK COLLECTION FOR SALE – Ben Finnegan is in the mood to sell his socks. All 22,000 pairs. Finnegan's been collecting socks from all over the world since he was a kid. Growing up an Army brat, he lived in 3 continents, and by the time he was 18 had amassed a collection of 8700 pairs, including a single rare Ethiopian sock from 1908, which was the last time anyone there actually wore socks. Sothebys' is deciding whether to handle the sale.

Some years back, Christie's handled the sale of the second largest sock collection, 18,500 pairs, at a time when most people in the know, believed that socks weren't selling, especially socks from other lands. It turned out to be one of the biggest successes that Christie's ever had. The collection had belonged to the Von Wurmser family of Germany, and had been passed down from father to son since the Middle Ages, when socks were first invented.

BUSICLANDER DISCOVERED IN BLARNEY CASTLE – An ancient Celtic musical instrument called the Busiclander, thought for many years to be as imaginary as the Unicorn, was actually found behind a secret door in the basement of Blarney Castle. Originally built in the year 1210, Blarney Castle is the most visited tourist attraction in Ireland, so it's amazing that no one had ever spotted this hidden room before. The Busiclander was considered a two man instrument, probably the only one in history. It was like a cross between the bagpipes, and a bassoon, but for some unknown reason was played in a sitting position, with a thin leather band tied tightly around the forehead, while an assistant simultaneously hummed along with the music .

Busiclander music was said to be some of the most beautiful music that Ireland had ever produced. According to legend, the instrument was originally named a "Musiclander," which literally meant "drawing the Clans together with music." However it became linked to a man known as the greatest Musiclander player of all time, and his name happened to be Busic. In his honor, the name of the instrument was changed to Busiclander, but amazingly none have ever been found until now.

MAN ROBS BANK USING PIECE OF PAPER—THREATENS TELLERS WITH NASTY PAPER CUTS – We all are well aware of how much a paper cut hurts. Well, a mild mannered accountant named Harvey Grindsberg went berserk and attempted to rob a bank using the edge of a piece of paper as a weapon. He threatened to inflict severe paper cuts on anyone who stood in his way. A sharp-eyed teller called the police, who came armed with automatic weapons. Realizing that the paper's edge was no match for their firepower, Grindsberg dropped his piece of paper, and gave up quietly.

Upon a subsequent search of his apartment, police found an arsenal of slingshots, water guns, and rubber bands with paper clips that he would shoot at people from his window. He also had bags of wet toilet paper that he pelted people with late at night as they walked past his residence. Sentenced to four years in prison, he hopes to be out of prison by next tax season, if he can get his sentence reduced for good behavior.

MAN CRUSHES HEAD IN GARBAGE COMPACTOR AND LIVES – George O'Doole admits having had a little too much to drink the night he peered into his garbage compactor to see what was clogging it up. The next thing he knew it was being further clogged up by his head. Doctors are amazed that not only did he survive that ordeal, but that all his senses still function, despite the fact that his head is now shaped like a cucumber

---

FARMER DISCOVERS NEW OCEAN USING A DIVINING ROD – A very surprised farmer in Idaho named Herb Stempel discovered what turned out to be a third North American ocean while searching for a place to dig a well. Trying an age-old technique of locating water using a divining rod, he found a lot more than he bargained for, and is now petitioning to have it called "Herb's Ocean." Imagine our national pride at having the Atlantic, the Pacific, and Herb's.

BOOK OF LIFE FOUND IN ISRAEL – Just in time for the Jewish New Year, a solid gold book has been found in a cave in Israel which Israeli archaeologists believe may be the actual Book of Life that was written about in the Old Testament.

Each year on Yom Kippur, which is known as The Day of Atonement, the Jewish people ask G-d for forgiveness for their transgressions during the previous year. They also ask for another year of life, and to have their names inscribed into The Book of Life.

The Book of Life was thought by many scholars to be metaphorical, or imaginary, because it was said to be written by G-d himself, and to contain every living person's name in the world, and the exact day they would die. Scholars always believed that such a book would have to be too huge to exist.

According to information leaked by a reliable source, this book is the size of a large family photo album, but is written in an ancient Aramaic type of code so tiny, only God could have written it. It is now being analyzed by the most sophisticated computers in the world.

ELDERLY MEN'S ROCK BAND SWEEPING THE U.K. – Four men in their 80s, and one who is 93, have taken the rock world by storm by forming a band called The Coots, and rising to the top of the charts in the U.K.. They are a true musical phenomenon.

They are definitely also the world's oldest living rock band. "We make The Stones look like children," says 93 year old Alistair Conley, who's Mick Jagger's senior by over 20 years, "but we still have the moves."

Amazingly, young girls in Britain are swooning over these old men. Three use walkers, and 2 have pacemakers, so they can't use electric guitars, because it might interfere with their heart rhythm. Eighty-six year old Emil Fontouche said, "It's such a crazy thing. My heart's the only part of me that doesn't have rhythm."

They seem to be patterning themselves after The Beatles. Where The Beatles sang, "I Wanna Hold Your Hand," The Coots sing, "I Have To Hold Your Hand."

MAN POLE-VAULTS ACROSS THE COUNTRY FOR CHARITY – Traveling 17 feet at a time is not the most expedient way to cross the country, unless you're 43 year old Albert Willigan, and you're trying to raise money for charity. Willigan had been a star pole vaulter in high school, and even though he hadn't done it in many years, he claims it still felt natural to him.

Kicking off with a running start in his hometown of Bellingham, Washington, Willigan carried only a backpack fastened to him with Velcro.

Unencumbered by not having to actually vault over a bar, he was able to make better time, as he was going not for height, but for distance.

The only exception was when he rented hotel rooms along the way, . . . always on the second floor, . . . so for publicity purposes, he would vault into his room through an open window.

He vaulted his way down into Idaho, then into Utah, where he pole-vaulted his way through Salt Lake City, and was welcomed by the Mormon population, who admired his determination, and energy-saving mode of travel.

While vaulting through Nashville, Tennessee, he was actually able to fulfill another life long dream, by recording a country western song entitled "You Built A Wall Around Your Heart, Till I Pole-Vaulted My Way Over It". It became an instant hit, and Willigan is now on his way to becoming a Country-Western star. Comparing himself to Jerry Lewis, who has never disclosed why he does the Muscular Dystrophy telethon every year, and refusing to divulge his motivation, he managed to raise the unbelievable sum of 4.4 million dollars, over the 9 month-long trip, leading other major charities to consider using pole-vaulting as a viable way of raising funds.

When it comes to successfully collecting funds for charity, Albert Willigan, has literally "raised the bar "in more ways than one.

SURGEON GENERAL SUGGESTS CO-WORKERS GIVE EACH OTHER PIGGY-BACK RIDES –Many corporate office workers never get a chance to get to the gym because they work such long hours. Lack of exercise can lead to illness, and lowered productivity, so Surgeon General Vitek Murthy, has come out with the suggestion that office workers give each other piggyback rides during their breaks, because as he says, "it's as close to a whole body workout as you can get without actually going to the gym, and also adds to office productivity by helping the workers get to know each other on a more intimate level. "

According to Murthy, a good, vigorous piggyback ride works your back, legs, arms, lats, shoulders, and especially your butt. It's also good for improving your balance.

He adds the admonition to always get the other person's approval before hoisting them up on your back, and to take into consideration what they're wearing as well. Women in very short skirts might feel that it's inappropriate, or even possibly a form of harassment to be forced to ride on a co-worker's back.

But once you ask permission, just grab a hold of the guy or gal next to you, get 'em up on your back, and gallop around the office. It's good for you! The Surgeon General said so!

U.N. PROPOSES SPELLING BEE TO SETTLE DISPUTES – In an astonishing display of how out of touch it really is, the United Nations has suggested settling international disputes through the use of a spelling bee. The General Assembly came up with a plan which they say will avoid the type of violence the world is now experiencing, by having the best spellers in each of the warring countries compete against each other in neutral territory.

They feel that most men who spell well are not prone to fighting, and they feel this can work, as long as the countries involved stick by their agreements to honor the winners of the spelling bee.

The proposed plan calls for the best spellers from each country to meet on neutral ground. Words will be provided by neutral countries with nothing to gain from either party having won.

Now they have to figure out what to do with countries that don't use letters, but use characters instead, like China and Japan. As far as the Middle East crisis goes, the Israelis are confident because they are known to be excellent spellers.

PRES. OBAMA STUDYING BALLET – To combat his drop in popularity in the polls, and in an effort to improve both his coordination and sense of confidence, the President's advisors have insisted he study ballet.

They have enrolled him in a public ballet class, which he faithfully attends with 11 little girls, ages 4 to 7, none of whom have any idea that "the tall boy" dancing with them is none other than the President of the United States.

He could certainly have taken private lessons, but because he has been slipping in the polls, his advisors felt that public lessons would make him seem more approachable, and more vulnerable, and would get him back his standing, as well as build up his confidence. The President is said to be excited about his first upcoming recital, in which he is expected to do a solo performance.

NEW HEADACHE REMEDY – Doctors at one of the major research hospitals have come up with a remarkable new way to relieve Migraine headaches, using a simple raisin. Take a black magic marker and make a dot in the center of your forehead. Now take a raisin, and press it directly into the dot with tremendous force. Hold that position for three to four minutes, and if you press hard enough, an ingredient in the raisin will pass through your skin, and alleviate the headache. If you don't have a raisin, try a lima bean.

VICE PRES. BIDEN HAS AN ALTER EGO – National Security Advisors are in an uproar over the rumor that Vice Pres. Joe Biden has an alter ego. Several reliable sources in Washington have reported seeing Biden showing up at parties wearing a loud plaid jacket, introducing himself to people as Fritz Pinn, a vaudeville comedian from the 40s. He then hands them a card that says, "My name may be Pinn, but I'm sharp as a tack," begins laughing hysterically, and slaps them on the back." There is concern over how this image will affect his standing in the international community, especially since he's mulling a run for President.

MAN ARRESTED FOR HAVING HIGH FEVER – A man in Georgia was arrested for having such a high fever that he began hallucinating. Just as it reached 106 degrees Fahrenheit, cops broke in and charged him with having an illegal fever, specifically for the purposes of hallucinating. The man was too sick to comment.

ELDERLY WOMEN'S MARATHON HELD IN NEW YORK CITY – The city of New York sponsored the very first Elderly Women's

Marathon, open to all women over the age of 75, and it was a huge success. The oldest competitor, 94 year old Rosa Biggs, from Tunesport, Tennessee, said she didn't even get into track and field events until her husband died when she was 82. "We lived on a farm," she said, "so after Ed passed, I began a little high jumping, using the bales of hay in the barn to break my fall. The only scandal marking the event was at the after-party, when two unidentified men in their 70s were caught dealing Ecstasy in the Men's Room, and were asked to leave.

The winner, 87 year old Emma Mae Twillits of Burlingham, New York, wore a specially made Nike outfit, including a sports thong, but instead of wearing sweat socks, she insisted on wearing her stockings rolled down around her ankles for good luck.

SOLO BALLROOM DANCING – When Abe Twaynish hits the dance floor for a wild and wooly Tango, or even for just a Waltz, or a simple Fox Trot, people stop what they're doing, and look, . . . and look, . . . and look.

Not just because he's so good at what he does, but because he does it all by himself. No partner. No props. "Just me, myself, and the dance-floor, and that's all she wrote," he says.

For more than 45 years, until just 2 years ago, Abe danced, and taught Ballroom Dancing with his lovely wife Gloria. When Gloria passed away suddenly while performing a particularly stressful backwards dip, Abe felt he would never dance again. He said, "She was so light on her feet for such a heavy woman!"

After six months of mourning, his friends and students urged him to continue dancing in Gloria's memory. But who would he choose as his partner?

He thought about it for months. Then one day, as if nothing had ever happened, Twaynish showed up at his dancing school, and made an announcement that he would be teaching a new form of ballroom dancing, … solo ballroom dancing. One person dancing alone, … no partner.

"This would be a lifesaver for lonely singles who otherwise would like to go out dancing, but have no partner," he explained. "Now they wouldn't need one."

Twaynish cautions about starting out too fast. "The twirls in some dances can be a killer, cause there's no one on the other side to slow you down. Even after all my years of experience, the first time I tried a Lindy Hop by myself, I got carried away, and spun myself right off the stage."

MEXICAN HAT DANCE ADOPTED BY SWEDEN – Until recently most every country had a national dance except Sweden. What most people don't know is that if a country doesn't use it's national dance for a certain number of years another country can claim it. Such is the case with Sweden and The Mexican Hat Dance. Upset over not having a national dance of it's own, Sweden has chosen to borrow the Mexican Hat Dance, since most Mexicans have not actually used that dance for over 112 years. Through a generous agreement, mediated by The United Nations, Sweden has gotten permission to use the dance, and is now in the process of importing approximately ten million sombreros, for the millions of Swedes who are excited to learn how to do it.

It was a Swedish politician, Sven Byern, who uncovered the ancient law that if a country did not use it's national dance in more than 75 years, it was basically up for grabs. It came down to a choice between the Flaming Sword Dance of Turkey, The Mexican Hat Dance, or the Myoog, the national dance of Bosnia, where the dancers put on music, crouch down low, and run towards each other full speed, until they bang heads. It is the only country where the national dance is performed strictly by men.

ANCIENT EGYPTIANS DID THEIR OWN DRY CLEANING – Archaeologists, and Egyptologists alike, are excited about the small, simple piece of parchment that was recently uncovered in a dig near Abu Simbel, one of the most famous of the ancient Egyptian sites. It turns out to be the earliest receipt for dry cleaning ever to be found in that part of the world. It was for three loincloths, a kalasiris, and 2 capes with no starch.

Noted Egyptologist, Dr. Hans Vrai said, "When you really stop to think about it, it's kind of sad. The man or woman this ticket belonged to probably never even got their clothing back."

He went on to say, "The reason this is such an important find is that we were always under the impression that the Egyptians sent their dry cleaning to the Kassites, who were known for being extremely neat, and were also known for settling in Babylonia and Mesopotamia. Now we believe that the embalming rooms, previously believed to be just used for mummification, were also used for dry cleaning purposes."

WOMAN CONVINCED SHE'S MARRIED TO A LIGHTBULB – Psychologists claim they've found a woman in Australia with the very rare condition known as "Filamental Psychosis" where sufferers believe they are emotionally involved with electrical appliances that have filaments.

Dr. Stew Shrevesport of Queensland, says that Margaret (Meg) Schwilling firmly believes she is married to a lightbulb. Schwilling confirms by saying,

"I met my "husband" at a dimly lit party several years ago, and just by his presence, he brightened up the entire room."

She continues, "In those days he was just a plain hundred watt bulb, but now that he's become a three-way bulb it's added a lot of excitement to our lives, and a whole new dimension to our sex life."

Shrevesport says in 30 years of practice, he'd never seen an actual case of Filamental Psychosis before, even though he'd read about it in many journals. "The closest I ever came to that," he said, "was the woman I treated who was infatuated with her sunlamp. But luckily for her, it turned out to be just a crush, and not a full fledged relationship."

SCHIZOPHRENIC POLICEMAN TAKES HIMSELF INTO CUSTODY – A police officer named Oslo Hertwig in Stuttgart, Germany marched himself into his local precinct, and asked to be arrested. He had himself in a wristlock, with one of his arms twisting the other arm behind his back, ostensibly "to keep himself from getting away," as he put it.

He explained that earlier in the day, he became suspicious of himself, when he noticed himself loitering in front of his apartment. When he confronted himself, and asked why he was there, he couldn't come up with an answer that satisfied him. When he ordered himself to leave, he refused, and stood his ground. That's when he identified himself as a police officer, and according to one bystander, "all Hell broke loose."

Anna May Shtoon, an eyewitness, described it like this. The officer threw himself down on the ground, and tried to get up on his own back. He just kept throwing punches even though he was yelling at himself to give up. Finally he overpowered himself, slapped on the cuffs, and led himself away.

His psychiatrist, Dr. Gerhart Meisterwald confirmed that Hertwig was a Paranoid-Schizophrenic, but said it was very unusual for someone with that condition to act out the way he did. "Usually," he said, "they are much more understanding of their behavior. It's just lucky he didn't pull his gun and shoot himself." Hertwig hired a lawyer, but then fired him for what he claimed was "double-billing."

TOP MODEL HAS ABDOMINAL ORGANS REMOVED FOR THINNER LOOK – Rumors have been flying for years about models doing bizarre things to enhance their looks, like extracting their back teeth, or having a rib or two removed.

But hot super model Evvie-Lou has gone one step, . . . make that ten steps, . . . further.

Rumor has it that she's actually had most of her abdominal organs removed, and now claims the smallest waist in the business, . . . a hair less than 12 inches.

Evvie-Lou the new international star of the Prime agency, with offices in New York, Paris, and L.A., shocked veteran fashion attendees at a show in Paris recently, when she showed up to model a line of low cut jeans, and the extra small size had to be taken in a full 8 inches, … and was still big on her.

Prime booker Hans Tragenbig says, "the phone has been ringing off the hook with people wanting to hire Evvie-Lou for every ad imaginable. No one has ever seen a body like that before. She's built like a wasp! Like she flew out of a hive."

Exercise guru Shmin Bedompta says "She makes Ghandi look obese."

When asked if she likes her new look, Evvie-Lou's current boyfriend, male model Jefferson Lee says, "I wish I could tell you differently, but she still thinks she's fat!"

MOSQUITO BITE SHOP OPENS IN PHILLY – Residents of North Philadelphia are now the proud owners of the country's first mosquito bite shop. Owner Horace Wilfrey explains, "lots of people in this neighborhood are embarrassed that they can't afford to go away on vacation during the summer. Now all that's changed. They come to me, I give them lots of mosquito bites, and then they can tell all their friends and neighbors that they went away to the country for the week-end, and nobody is any the wiser. I'm over-run with business, and starting next week, I'll also be selling Calamine Lotion!"

IRAQI POLICE TAUGHT TO USE JOKES TO LOWER CRIME RATE – When used properly, humor has been known to calm even the most violent offenders, and now it is being used to lower the crime rate in Iraq. Statistics from the U.S. Army show that Baghdad , rated as the most dangerous city in the world, now has a murder rate lower than New York City, and the main reason for that is comedy.

Thanks to a U.S. policy known as "Operation HaHa," police in Iraq, as well as other trouble spots in the world, are being forced to work with stand-up comedians, learning to use humor to help defuse potentially life-threatening situations.

Achmed Haboubi, an officer in the Iraqi police force said he prefers to use jokes about crime, and keeps several in his repertoire. He said one of his favorites is, "Crime was so bad in Iraq, I went to visit a friend in the hospital, and I got mugged by a doctor. I could tell he was a doctor because he wiped my neck off with alcohol before he put the knife to my throat." Through paroxysms of laughter, he added, "the last guy I told that joke to laughed so hard, he dropped his bomb."

MUSICAL TOILET PAPER – Doctors who treat stress know that many of their patients spend a lot of time in the bathroom, as stress can lead to conditions like Irritable Bowel Syndrome and the like. Dr. Emanuel Hertwig, a gastrointestinal specialist at the University of Laden in Austria, has come up with an idea he claims can solve all that, musical toilet paper.

Dr. Hertwig explains it like this, "As the paper winds off the roll, it starts a motor-like drive, similar to the action of the old player-pianos so popular in 19th and early 20th century Austria.

The next thing you know, soothing New Age music begins to play by itself, and fills the room with healing sound. Patients love it. The more they visit the bathroom, the calmer they get."

OBESE US CITIZENS DONATE FAT TO THIRD WORLD COUNTRIES

– The United States was named the obesity capital of the world according to the annual survey done by the government's office on Health Affairs. The survey states that more than 61% of adults currently fall into the category of obesity, defined as having a BMI, (Body Mass Index) of 25 or over.

OPOA, (Obese People of America), a society that endeavors to put a positive spin on being obese, counters that claim by saying that people who are obese tend to be more generous, and to prove that fact, they are asking their members to donate some of their own body fat to poor people around the world. Liposuction units are being assembled to collect the fat, which will then be injected into starving people in many third world countries. Hattie Lumbacker, current President of OPOA said, "They may still be poor, but at least they'll all be nice and fat."

CONGRESSMEN PLAY HIDE AND SEEK

– For the most part, it is a well kept secret that many public servants wind up in psychotherapy due to the stress of their jobs. GNN has discovered a secret White House directive that suggests that Senators and members of the House of Representatives engage in more recreational activities, in order to help them handle the stress inherent to their work. Those "recreational activities" have apparently turned out to be common street games.

An anonymous inside source reports that "very often after a strenuous debate, Senators and Congressmen alike take a break, and go outside into the courtyard for a bipartisan no-holds barred game of "Hide and Seek." He admits that the Democrats usually are the best players, because, according to him, "they tend to be the best at hiding things."

The elected officials come back sweaty, and tired, but so emotionally refreshed that they're thinking of adding Ringalivio, Skelly, and Eagle and the Rats to the mix.

MAN CRAWLS ACROSS THE UKRAINE

– In a tribute to his disabled brother Yoneg, who has spent all his life in a wheelchair, Yushnev Plintz crawled across the Ukraine in a period of 14 months, and at a cost of 78 pairs of pants.

Beginning his crawl on a balmy September day, in the city of Uzhorod on the Slovakian border, Plintz ended his historic crawl on a cold, rainy day in November, a year and two months later, by crawling into the town of Kharkiv near the Russian border. He was literally on his last pair of pants.

He explained, "Before my crawl began, I had raised enough money through donations to buy just 78 pairs of pants, with reinforced knees. I guess God knew exactly how many I would need."

When asked why he attempted this amazing feat in the first place Plintz said, "People given the gift of mobility have no idea what it feels like not to be able to get around. I made this crawl in solidarity with all people who are in Yoneg's position." He said that in English, but with a very heavy accent.

Since most of the Ukraine consists of fertile plains, and plateaus, Plintz said the crawling was easier than he expected. He made sure to avoid the Carpathian Mountains, as he explained, "no one as yet has been able to crawl The Carpathians, and I was so determined to succeed, I didn't want to give myself a totally insurmountable task."

"I also made sure to avoid The Black Sea," he added almost tongue in cheek.

REDWOOD TREE GROWS IN COUPLE'S APARTMENT – Talk about earth colors. Dora and Harry Swalloon woke up one morning to find what looked like a tree growing right in the middle of their living room out of their brown shag carpeting. They began watering it, and to their amazement, over the next few months, it grew into a huge redwood tree. Having become a money-making tourist attraction, the Swalloons think it's a sign from God.

FEMINISTS INSIST UPON GRANDMOTHER CLOCKS – Crashing through yet one more sociological barrier, California feminists have insisted on the making of Grandmother clocks, as well as Grandfather clocks. They state that historically, women are more likely to be on time than men, and are more deserving of having a large clock named after them. Clock makers are puzzled as to how to determine the exact gender of a clock. They are considering building a "skirt" around the lower half.

CELEBS. CONFER WITH DEAD DWARF – Forget Ramtha, Seth, and Melchizedek. Mediums in California claim they are currently channeling the spirit of Oppo, a dead dwarf who supposedly lived in Ancient Egyptian times. He was thought to have had the power to see into the future. He predicts that within the next 50 years, all men will walk in a low crouching walk, like Groucho Marx did in his films.

WOMAN SO BEAUTIFUL SHE HAS TO TRAVEL WITH PARAMEDICS – Beauty can either be a gift or a curse. In the case of Magda Soto it's a toss-up. She is so incredibly beautiful, she has to travel with paramedics to revive men who look at her for too long. She needs to take out special insurance, and when she goes to the beach, she's forced to carry a warning sign with her, "Men with pacemakers, don't look!"

RARE VIRUS SWEEPS JAPAN, VICTIMS TOO WEAK TO BOW – A bizarre type of virus swept through Japan this past week afflicting thousands of people with high fevers, stomach disorders, and back pain. Most victims were left too weak to bow, and were forced to try and greet each other by shaking hands, which many in the government looked down upon as being "too Western."

SCREW-ON HATS – Plastic surgeons and toothpaste manufacturers in Chicago, have gotten together to create a screw-on hat, solving an age old problem in The Windy City, where men have been losing hats to strong gusts of wind for as long as people can remember. "This hat will stay on even in a hurricane," say the inventors. A plastic surgeon creates very subtle ridges under your hair encircling your head, with matching ridges in the hats so they can screw on like a toothpaste cap.

CLUB FOR SHY GANGSTERS – Many gangsters are forced to travel a lot, and often report feeling quite alone on the road. This often leads to depression, and more violence than might be necessary when they reach their destination. Not anymore. Dr. Harwell Grobear of Yale has suggested creating social clubs where gangsters might meet other nice gangsters, in a more social environment. Law officials feel that if the gangsters are happier while on the road, they will be less prone to violence when they get where they're going.

DENTISTS RECOMMEND SQUEEZING FOOD FOR THE ELDERLY – Many dentists have elderly patients with badly worn dentures who can't afford to get new ones, and their digestion suffers because they can't chew their food well. A dentist in Arkansas has suggested teaching the elderly to squeeze their food first, before eating it. He suggests starting with something simple like a tunafish sandwich, squeezing it tightly in their hands, and passing it back and forth from one hand to the other, until it's finely squeezed, making it easier to digest. The American Dental Association is weighing this recommendation.

MAN IMPALED ON SPIKE, STILL SHOWS UP FOR WORK ON TIME – Herb Stemp was incredibly proud of his attendance record at work, having never been late during the thirty seven years he labored as an artichoke stuffer. Accidentally impaling himself on a spike one Sunday almost spoiled his perfect record, but to his surprise, when emergency workers separated the spike from the fence where he had fallen, he found that the spike wasn't that uncomfortable, and he opted to wait until his next day off to have it removed. His main complaint was that his jacket didn't close properly.

TRAMPOLINES FOR THE ELDERLY – The Surgeon General came out with a new report that claims that elderly people would benefit from daily workouts on a trampoline. Not only would it be good for their circulation, but the jumping would shake up their internal organs, which tend not to get much exercise. The science behind this story is backed up by the story of the elderly man who pogo-sticked across Europe.

ARTIFICIAL TREES SPROUT REAL FRUIT–SEEN AS SIGN FROM GOD – The Garden of Eden, an artificial tree outlet in Bangor, Maine, legendary home of Paul Bunyan, has people lining up for miles to see what some people are referring to as a sign from God.

Besides the usual Christmas trees on sale at this time of year, Felice and Norberto Findelspain, the Adam and Eve of the establishment, have always advertised the largest assortment of artificial trees in the surrounding area, but until this past week, none of the trees bore fruit.

Norberto says, "when I came in last Tuesday morning, I thought one of my employees was playing some sort of joke on me, but it was no joke. All my trees had luscious looking fruit growing off of them. I pulled off an apple and couldn't believe how juicy and delicious it was. Obviously only God could do something like that."

People have been traveling in from surrounding states to see and buy these amazing trees, which Findelspain has been pricing at $350 per tree, as he puts it, "a small price to pay to own a miracle."

As far as care goes, Findelspain has little in the way of instructions. "I don't think you need to water them," he said, "because I'm not even sure where you would put it."

So far, the trees have been growing apples, cherries, and oranges. Findelspain thinks God chose him to use as a sign that He can accomplish anything, because he has always been honest with his customers, and tried to lead a good life.

6" TALL TRIBE FOUND IN AFRICA— MAKE PYGMIES LOOK LIKE GIANTS – A race of 6 inch tall, perfectly formed native Africans was discovered living on Kubu Island in Botswana. The children are anywhere from two to three inches tall, and the babies are about half an inch long when born. They live in small pyramid shaped mud huts, speak an unknown language, and seem to be fierce warriors. They make pygmies look like giants.

ABE LINCOLN WAS A PATHOLOGICAL LIAR – Abe Lincoln had the reputation of being known as "Honest Abe," but according to a diary discovered by GNN, written by Abigail Lawrence, an ex-girlfriend of his, Abe was the worst liar in the world. "The honesty thing was all done for publicity," she said, "because if people knew the real Abe, he would never have been elected."

SOCKS WITH HEELS AND LACES – A company in California claims to have revolutionized the haberdashery world by inventing leather socks with heels and laces. Shoe salesman are in an uproar, claiming that these so-called socks are just rip-offs of shoes with no socks, and that the gullible public is falling for it.

PITCHER THROWS WORLD'S FASTEST FAST-BALL – A new pitcher from The Dominican Republic named Orlando Vincent threw a fastball that was clocked at an amazing 208 miles per hour. Not only did it break the catcher's wrist, but it burnt a hole in his glove as well. Opposing players are complaining about getting up to bat, and are afraid for their lives.

IGLOO COLLAPSES IN MANHATTAN – The Snave family, a homesick family of Eskimos can thank their lucky stars today. It seems their trouble all started when they tried to make Manhattan into Alaska, and built a huge igloo using large blocks of ice they obtained from a local fish market. The father, a physics professor, devised an internal cooling system that kept the ice from melting, but in a recent blackout, the system failed, and the igloo collapsed trapping the entire family under tons of ice. Fortunately for them a certain Mr. Blinken came along carrying an ice-pick, and within moments somehow freed the entire family. I think it's certainly safe to say that Mr. A. Blinken will always be remembered as "the man who freed The Snaves."

EXTRA-TERRESTRIAL RACE OF TINY AMPHIBIOUS BEINGS INVADING EARTH THROUGH OUR TOILET BOWLS – Scientists at NASA have long tried to deny the existence of other life forms here on Earth, but now they have no choice but to admit it. Marine Biologist Harry Langsdon has identified the presence of tiny amphibious beings with human–like heads surfacing in people's toilet bowls all around the world. Very often they disguise themselves as small yellow kernels of corn. Langsdon advises to just keep flushing until you're sure they're gone.

CHIROPRACTORS ADVISE WEARING SWIM FINS FOR BACK PAIN – Something about the stability of wearing swim fins seems to relieve the painful, debilitating symptoms of sciatica. Chiropractors all over the country have been advising their patients to wear swim fins to the office, especially if their job involves a lot of standing. One cardiac surgeon was reported to be wearing fins in the operating room, and several cops have been seen wearing them while assigned to long stake-outs.

THE FABULOUS FLYING NAFE TWINS TAKE THE CIRCUS WORLD BY STORM – Henri and Albert Nafe of Paris, France are twin dwarf acrobats who have the incredibly rare ability to swing from a trapeze bar by their tongues. Blessed with abnormally long tongues, the twin dwarves keep their tongues strong by doing one hundred tongue push-ups a day.

CANADIAN REPAIR-MAN WAKES UP WITH FRENCH ACCENT – The wife of a Canadian toaster repair-man named Herb Trirt claims they've never done any traveling, so when her husband awoke one morning, addressed her as "mon cherie ," and asked for a croissant, in a heavy French accent she thought he was kidding. Not only that, she said, "he's begun wearing a beret, grew a thin moustache, and began using a walking stick."

"It's as if suddenly I'm becoming French against my will" Trirt said. "I'm even taking a dislike to Americans, and becoming intolerant of other people's backgrounds." He claims it all started after receiving a shock from one of his damaged toasters.

ANCIENT CAVE DRAWINGS FOUND OF PRESIDENT OBAMA – Ain Sokhna Road,Egypt -Only 25 miles from Cairo, ancient sacred cave drawings were found dating back to 7000-6500 B.C. that seem to show an exact likeness of President Barack Hussein Obama dressed in ancient Egyptian garb. Verne Sackler of Utah, happened to be looking for souvenirs to bring back home, when he accidentally stumbled on the find of the century. Scientists and Egyptologists have confirmed the likeness of Pres. Obama appearing many times on the sacred walls. It appears he was some kind of High Priest or may even have been a Pharaoh. It is hoped that this will serve to help him bring about peace in the Middle East.

SCIENTISTS DISCOVER REAL FOUNTAIN OF YOUTH IN BRAZIL – When people used to go to Brazil to get younger looking, it was because they went to super plastic surgeon to the stars, Ivo Pitanguy. Now they go to drink the water. Scientists from NIH have discovered an entire village made up of only teens and 20-somethings that have birth certificates that show they're actually in their 70s, and 80s. Their only explanation is that the well water in their village is the real fountain of youth. It even works on animals. All the dogs and cats are puppies and kittens. They are expected to bring the water back to the United States for study.

SPEEDREADER READS 500 BOOKS A WEEK – Devlin, Indiana – Ida Bewletts, 48 years old, can't stop reading. She perfected her own technique of speed-reading to the point that she can read 500 books a week. That breaks down to an amazing 71.42 books a day. The government is training her to read classified documents. She claims to only need 3 hours of sleep a night, and reads voraciously, night and day. She remembers almost everything she reads, as she also has a photographic memory. She's read every book in her town's library 3 times.

CONTORTIONIST GETS LOOSE IN WHITE HOUSE – In yet another embarrassment to the Secret Service, a 40 year old, female contortionist/ circus performer, named Emma Lopane , cornered Pres. Obama, while on a tour of The White House, and performed for him privately before she was arrested. Secret Service was afraid she was a terrorist, and might try to strangle him with her legs. They took her out tied in a knot.

MAN SPEAKS EVERY LANGUAGE IN THE WORLD – Helmut Schving of Latvia has the rare gift of "Photographic Lingualism". All he has to do is hear part of any language once, and he can automatically figure out the rest. Even the rare dialects of China and India. He's currently working on ancient languages that have been considered dead for many years, and can also translate hieroglyphs just by looking at them. He's being hired by the U.N. because he's like a one man General Assembly.

WOMAN GIVES BIRTH TO SERVICE FOR 12 – Atlanta, Georgia – Doctors at Maimonides Hospital of Atlanta were shocked and amazed when a clanking noise was heard as Monique Swiggins gave birth to an entire set of fine silverware instead of the twins she and her husband were expecting.

Dr. Herbert Cronk, her obstetrician said that in all his years delivering babies, he's never seen anything like it.

He said he had read unconfirmed reports that a woman in Somalia once gave birth to a toaster, and that a woman in Guadeloupe-Hidalgo gave birth to an assortment of fine china, but to his knowledge neither case had ever actually been verified.

He claims the Swiggins' offered to let him adopt a particularly lovely cake knife, but that he turned them down because something about it "just didn't seem right."

The first trimester of pregnancy is the most critical in terms of the developing fetus, said Cronk, and many women obsess over certain things during that period.

Swiggins said that all throughout her first trimester, she had been obsessing over what to buy her sister for her upcoming wedding, and had been looking through catalogues of silverware, trying to decide on a pattern.

She finally settled on Grand Baroque, which amazingly was the exact pattern of the flatware she gave birth to.

Her husband Dwight said he was willing to make the best of the situation, and wondered if he could look forward to seeing the teaspoons grow up and become tablespoons.

GIANT SQUID FOUND IN MAN'S TOILET—TENTACLE MEETS TESTICLE – Montgomery, Alabama – Elbert Scruggs was answering nature's call when he got the surprise of his life.

The way he tells it, "I was sittin' on the throne, readin' the comics, when all of a sudden I felt somethin' latch onto my privates, … like a suction cup. The pain was excruciating. I looked into the bowl, and was shocked to see a long winding arm with suckers all over it comin' out of the water, wrapped around my what-sis. It was tryin' to pull me under."

Scruggs managed to pull away, and tied the tentacle to one of the legs of his sink with a length of rope, before running out onto the road screaming, with his pants around his ankles.

Harold Nadkin of the Animal Preservation Society arranged for a marine biologist to investigate Scruggs' toilet, and decided it had been a giant squid.

Nadkin surmised, "Someone must have thrown a baby squid into the sewer system, and somehow it survived, and grew into adult size. One of it's tentacles made it's way into Scruggs' toilet. He's lucky he didn't lose his sexual parts," said Nadkin.

TWIN TERRORISTS HURL THEMSELVES ACROSS OUR BORDER BY SLINGSHOT – Montreal, Canada – Canadian authorities have announced the arrest of two terrorists who happen to be identical twins, Mohammed El Zayeek, and Zayeek El Mohammed of Tunisia.

The two men attempted to fling themselves over the U.S. border with a huge slingshot made from two trees, and the biggest rubber band anyone had ever seen. The CIA has issued a warning that others may try this approach, once tried by an American nightlife impresario to try and make a big entrance at the opening of a new hotel, which ended up in disaster. The CIA went on to explain that certain documents found in Kabul detail a terrorist plot to fling terrorists into this country by slingshot.

MAN ARRESTED FOR ORDERING NON-EXISTENT FOOD – Practical joker Jack Lambo ordered food with made-up names and then complained bitterly when told they didn't have it. After the 16th time he ordered Twirn with a side order of Nashpes, he was arrested, and taken to a real jail, where he had to eat whatever they gave him.

RARE BREED OF FLYING CATS DISCOVERED IN SUMATRA – The jungles of Sumatra seem to have given birth to a heretofore unknown breed of cat that has the ability to fly when it feels threatened. Looking basically like house cats, the flying felines seem to sprout wings and take off at the first sign of danger. Coincidentally, there are no small birds in Sumatra.

REAL LIFE RAPUNZEL CHARGED IN PRISON BREAK – Theta Bientz had already been in the Guinness Book of World Records for having the longest hair in the world, 18 feet in length, by the time she wound up in jail for assault. Jethro Turner was also serving time, and could have been said to have the shortest hair in the world, as he was totally bald. They were both locked up in a minimum security prison and were believed to have been in a relationship. She helped him escape by letting him climb down her hair.

FUTURE STORIES

Man Who Got A Job As A Revolving Door

Man Puts Seashell To His Ear, And Drowns

Man Goes For Cataract Surgery Winds Up With X-Ray Vision

Goldfish Won At Carnival Grows Into A Whale

Man Who Digests Metal

Chimp Does Dentistry

Man Discovers Cure For All Diseases In His Basement

Man Stays Awake For 3 Weeks Straight

Man With No Formal Education Discovers New Antibiotic At Home

Teenager Who Can Run 35 Mph

Surgeon Arrested For Doing Heart Surgery At A Party

Man Sued For Using Handkerchief Without A License

Man Gets Rich By Asking Everyone In The World For A Penny

Man Arrested For Giving His Daughter The Name Snaydelbyune

Men Who Use Their Tie As A Pointer

Men Who Try To Pay For Things With Empty Video Boxes

Man Chokes To Death Trying To Speak French

Man Strangles Victims With His Hair

Scientists Create Human Termites To Combat Famine—Now They Can Eat Wood

Man Slides Into Home Base, And Disappears

ACKNOWLEDGMENTS

No book, or any creative project for that matter gets done by only one person, and this project was no different. Thanks are in order to Debbie Herman and Joshua Adams for believing in this project that I've been wanting to do for such a long time, and for allowing me to bring it to fruition, to the talented Jane McWhorter for her beautiful design work, to Scott Dikkers for writing such a cool foreword and for carrying on the tradition of spreading unusual news by creating "The Onion," and to my illustrator Dylan Clancy for his artistic talent and his ability to grasp the comedic aspect of each story and bring it to life with his amazing drawings. In short, he totally gets it!

I also want to thank my parents Marge and Ray Gurian for giving me my sense of humor, … that as it is, … and the encouragement to always follow my dreams, and to my two amazing daughters Elizabeth and Kathryn who unfortunately for them had to grow up listening to stories like these but fortunately still turned out okay! And now they get to share them with their own children, … whether they want to or not! So big shout-outs to Nicky, Lilly, Brookie and Adri because I think this book can be enjoyed by people of all ages. It's kind of like a children's book for adults, … if the adults are really childish!

Dylan Clancy is a multidisciplinary artist endangering the prestige of fine arts one medium at a time — including design :) animation :) : P and the written word, " :) ." When he's not collaborating with brilliant creators you can find him pursuing his own projects on his site SaxoLaxo.com.

Jeffrey Gurian is a comedy writer, performer, director, author, producer, doctor and Healer. He's written material for comedy legends such as Rodney Dangerfield, Joan Rivers, George Wallace, Phil Hartman, Richard Belzer, and Andrew "Dice" Clay, among many others. Jeffrey has performed stand-up at most of the big clubs in N.Y. and L.A. and was featured several times on Comedy Central's hit Kroll Show with Nick Kroll, John Mulaney, Amy Poehler, Seth Rogen, Laura Dern and Katy Perry. He was in the viral "Too Much Tuna" sketch and is also a regular on-air personality on Sirius XM's Bennington Show, where he also brings on special guests/friends like Russell Peters, Trevor Noah, Colin Quinn, Artie Lange, Susie Essman, D.L. Hughley, and Lisa Lampanelli. He writes a weekly column covering the comedy scene for The Interrobang called "Jumping Around With Jeffrey Gurian," and has also written for MTV, *National Lampoon*, *Weekly World News* and many Friars Roasts.

In 1999 he launched *Comedy Matters*, a celeb-based online entertainment column that has evolved into Comedy Matters TV, an internet TV channel with over 400 A-list celebrity interviews and well over one million views. He's produced shows starring Kevin Hart and Susie Essman, and according to Paul Provenza is known by everyone in comedy.

He was honored to have been given his own column in the legendary Weekly World News called "Gurian's World of the Bizarre." That led to the creation of GNN (Gurian News Network) which brings you the most unusual stories in The Universe, missed by mainstream media. He claims to have not slept in many years in order to bring these stories to light! GNN is definitely your source for "All The News That's Fit To Dance To," . . . hence *Man Robs Bank With His Chin!* Enjoy!!!

For more on Jeffrey and GNN visit Jeffrey's website at:
http://www.comedymatterstv.com

On Twitter and Instagram it's @jeffreygurian

Printed in Great Britain
by Amazon